PRAISE FOR T

"One of my favorite books s~~o~~
and, oh, the lust radiating off ~~or our heroes . . . I definitely recommend this~~
series for lovers of all things paranormal and awesome." **–USA Today**

"Robson's blend of smart-alecky wit, good old-fashioned romance, and suspenseful episodes of fighting off evil spirits form a paranormal thriller that will make pulses pound." **–Publishers Weekly**

"I would devour anything that Ms. Robson writes. I strongly recommend [the Weird Girls] series to PNR/UF readers and fans of Larissa Ione, Kresley Cole and Gena Showalter. Cecy Robson is pretty up there, IMO." **–Under the Covers Book Blog**

When I started reading the Weird Girls series a few years back, I fell deeply in love with Cecy Robson's sharp, funny dialogue, hilarious characters and brilliant world building. **–Book and Movie Dimension**

"I love this series! It is funny, action filled, and filled with hot para awesomeness." **–Delphina Reads Too Much**

"[Of Flame and Light] Most action-packed/thrilling/unputdownable book of the year [2016] and Best Sequel and Series Ender...Tara Wird – most memorable character of 2016." **–The Reading Cave**

"[With Robson's] edgy, witty and modern style of storytelling, the reader will be drawn deep into this quirky paranormal world. . . Strong pacing, constant action and distinctive, appealing characters—including a gutsy heroine—will no doubt keep you invested." **–RT Book Reviews**

"A healthy dose of humor, a heaping dash of the supernatural, and a pinch of mystery all laced with a heavy dollop of action . . . Robson knows how to combine all the best ingredients to keep her readers hooked and begging for another hit." **–Fresh Fiction**

"...Robson's supernatural tale will leave readers clawing for the next installment." —**Booklist**

"Page after page it's packed with non-stop action, a lot of conflicts and well-developed characters. The Weird Girls is a fast-paced read, one I can guarantee you, you won't be able to put down." —**The Bookaholic Cat**

"I was blown away by the depth of passion, humor, and creativity in this story...If you are a fan of powerful, sarcastic heroines and cross-over urban fantasy / paranormal romance stories, I highly recommend *Of Flame and Light*." —**Grave Tells Romance**

"Why do I love this series so much? Ms. Robson is a master at blending hilarious humor and scorching romance with her imaginative crazy action and fight scenes." —**Addicted to Happily Ever After**

In Too Far Novels
Salvatore

Death Seeker Novels
Unearthed

APPS
Crazy Maple's Chapters: Interactive Stories APP:
Shattered Past, Weird Girls and O'Brien Family Series

Hooked – Chat stories APP:
Cecy Robson writes as Rosalina San Tiago

Touch of Evil

of Evil

A WEIRD GIRLS NOVEL

INTERNATIONAL & AWARD-WINNING AUTHOR

CECY ROBSON

Published in the United States by Cecy Robson, LLC.

Cover design © Rebecca Weeks, Dark Wish Designs
Copy Edits by Sean Kelly
Proofreading by James Robson
Formatting by Jesse Gordon, A Darned Good Book

eBook ISBN # 978-1-947330-35-1
Print ISBN # 978-1-947330-36-8

DEDICATION

To Patty, Ilona and Gordan, and to Jim,
for giving me magic to believe in.

ACKNOWLEDGMENTS

As an author, I have written many novels. Like, a lot of novels. When I think back to how much time I've invested, all the tears I've cried onto my keyboard, and all the crazy dialogue that's made me laugh as I type, it's awesome to think how many readers have laughed and cried along with me. All those moments where I have clutched my heart, wondering who was going to live, die—all those times when I was genuinely terrified —y'all were right there with me. So, thank you, readers, fans, my beloved and dedicated followers who crack up, scream, and agonized right along with me. You're the reason I'm on this wild ride. And yes, finally Emme and Bren are here!

To my agent, Nicole Resciniti, you are my champion. You hustle and fight for me and while I thank you, I don't think you'll ever grasp the extent of my gratitude.

To Jamie, my partner in life and in business. Babe, I'm not sure how you put up with me, but you do, and somehow keep smiling. Thank you for thinking "Bren" is hilarious. I think "he" is, too.

To my assistant and publicist Kimberly Costa from your advice, to your support, to your willingness to read my words over and over (did I mention over?) again.

To Kristin Clifton, you started out as a reviewer, you became a fan, now, you are a friend. Thank you for reading my work.

To Sean Kelly, I asked you to edit and look, here, you are!

To Rebecca Weeks for the lovely cover and fast work. Thank you for your patience and your magic.

And once more to my fans. You asked for Emme and Bren. At last, they're finally here.

Chapter One

Emme

There's a naked werewolf standing in front of me.

Let me kindly explain.

There's *a naked werewolf*—a man who can *change* into a wolf—standing naked, in human form, in front of me.

They do that a lot, *change* from beast to full naked glory. Typically, it's pre and post bloody battle for the sake of the world and to protect its unsuspecting human populace. However awkward, I'm used to it.

"Like what you see?" he asks.

Make that sort of used to it.

He flexes and gives a little thrust to show off what he thinks are some delectable goods and *oh, my*...he has three testicles.

I slap my hands over my eyes. I take it back. I take it all back. I'm not used to all *this*.

"Emme," Ted asks. "Did you just gag?"

I'm not a rude person.

I'm not a liar.

"Yes?" is my response.

Ted is a lot bigger than me. He's also stronger and can snap my spine without *changing* to his beast counterpart. I keep my hands over my eyes. As a nurse by trade, and a supernatural fighter by sheer terrible luck, I have seen things. Ugly, frightening, and unexceptionally evil things. And I've encountered creatures so menacing mere thoughts reduce me to trembles.

I draw the line at extra testicles.

The sound of slapping and bouncing skin causes me to shrink inward. Ted seems to be putting on quite the show. Honestly, it sounds like a one-man juggling act involving best-left-covered body parts.

I'm tired of dating Teds.

And humans, they wouldn't survive me or the world my sisters and I were thrown into.

No, in order to be with me you must have something special.

And I'm not referring to what Ted is currently playing with.

My hands slip away from my face when I sense his approach.

"In my world, I'm revered for my virility," he says to my back.

"Mm-hmm," I reply. I pity the packmate forced to run behind him.

Ted is either referring to his obscenely large member *weres* are known for ("They're built for attracting females," my perky sister once explained) or the extra semen sack dangling halfway down his thigh. Neither impress me and neither does Ted.

I carefully step over the second of two discarded pizza boxes and make my way toward the exit.

My steps slow as I reach the door.

I turn to my left, then to my right. Something else is here.

Dread and resentment drag their long spindly fingers across my skin and hate coats my tongue.

I'm scared and on guard, and it's not because of Ted.

My gaze skips around the apartment, past the galley kitchen and to the boarded window covered with a *Scarface* poster. I don't see anyone or anything else. What I sense though is wrong and it shouldn't be here.

I keep my voice quiet, not wanting whatever is here to hear me. "Do you feel that?" I ask.

"Yeah, baby," he says. "It feels good. How about you feel it, too?"

Forget it. Ted is on his own.

TOUCH OF EVIL · 13

I grip the greasy knob, trying not to give too much thought as to why it's greasy, and more than anxious to leave Ted and his new roommate behind.

Ted slams his hand on the door above my head. It's a show of strength, reminding me that he's the one with the muscles and no matter how hard I pull, this door won't open unless he allows it.

Hot and heavy breath skitters along my neck, fluttering the strands of loose blonde hair that escaped my bun. He's aroused, like a wolf who's just caught his prey.

Except I'm not prey, no matter how much I resemble the part.

"I thought you were different, Emme," he whispers, this tenor pitch dropping low.

My hand slips away from the knob. "I thought you were different, too," I say.

There were no penis pics from Ted. No midnight booty calls while drunk on witch's brew. No inappropriate texts that made me blush or had me Googling terms like "pony play."

I did think Ted was different. Yet here I am, in a dirty apartment and in the company of another naked loser and...something else.

That sense of hate returns, surging along with a foreboding air of vengeance. Whatever is here is out for blood.

Ted skims his knuckles down my spine, adding another layer of "ew" with each pass. But it's that feeling that we're not alone that amplifies my need to escape.

I reach for the knob, again. It's useless, Ted keeps his position and the door firmly in place.

"You're making this a lot harder than it needs to be," I tell him. My eyes fix on the chipped gray paint covering the wood. Ted is under the impression he has me where he wants me. He fails to see I'm the one in control.

"You're the so-called 'sweet' one," Ted begins. "The innocent one of the Weird girls."

The insult draws my attention back to him. "Our last name is Wird," I correct. "And we're not a fan of that nickname."

Ted continues as if I never spoke. "I know better. Every hetero with a dick does. You fucked that vampire and fucked him good, no?"

His Creole accent was cute at first. Nothing of that cuteness remains. Heat builds along my cheeks, erasing the chills that the dark presence stirred.

My teeth clench hard. "You don't know what you're talking about."

"I also hear you're sad and lonely, desperate since your boyfriend was killed. You remember him, don't you? The same *were* who preferred a disfigured freak over you—"

I whip around, no longer feeling polite. "Don't you dare speak of Liam and his mate that way, and don't presume to know me."

"Relax, sugar tits. They can't hear me. They're dead, remember?"

I slap him across the face. It hurts. *Oh, it hurts.* I avoid shaking out the burn in my hand. The strike worked against me. He barely felt it. But he knows I felt his words.

Humiliation crawls across my face. Being *were,* he can sniff my pain and embarrassment. He laughs, bent on casting another blow. "Your brother-in-law is the Alpha Aric Connor, right chérie?"

The throbbing pain stiffening my fingers tightens my response. "Yes."

Aric is a revered pureblood and the strongest of his kind. His reputation alone cautions supernaturals against offending me. Ted, being new to Tahoe and naïve to Aric's power, doesn't understand he's about to cross a very dangerous line.

He bends to meet my face, his lascivious grin cutting lines into his narrow face.

"Just because you're related to the alpha by marriage doesn't make you anything special. If you want the truth, it's your sister Taran I wanted. She's as hot as the fire she casts with her magic. If she wasn't mated to the second in command, I would have fucked her harder than you did that vamp." He pushes off the door. "Now, run away, little girl. Keep living your lonely and pathetic life. Maybe next time, you'll appreciate the piddly scraps thrown your way."

Angry tears threaten to fall and sizzle across my burning face. His tirade struck almost every insecurity I possess.

Some beings make an art of out of inflicting pain. Ted should run a master class.

I square my shoulders. "It's one thing to not take rejection well," I say. "It's another to be cruel to spare your ego."

Ted shrugs. "Not cruel, chérie. *Honest.*" He straightens to his full height to look further down his long nose at me. "You're lucky," he says. "I don't usually waste my time with weaklings like you."

I blink back the tears I'm tired of shedding. "No, *you're lucky* I don't throw you out the window."

This really makes him laugh.

He stops laughing when I do, in fact, throw him out the window.

My *force*, the cool name my bubbly sister nicknamed my telekinetic power, funnels from my core and propels Ted and his might-mighty ego across the room. What remains of the boarded window explodes into shards of glass and splintering wood.

Ted lands with a thud, and plenty of swearing, three stories below with leftover window bits raining down on him.

I turn the knob and step into the open stairwell of Ted's apartment building, pausing when a warning pokes at me and reminds me I'm not alone.

The door shuts behind me with a creak. I look down the hall. To my right, only quiet awaits, the only signs of life from the reflection of a T.V. against a window. My way out is a different story.

A *were*, bear I believe, rests his back against a wall, speaking to what might be a cougar. I'm not like my sister Celia, whose inner tigress can scent a predator, or like Taran, who can distinguish supernaturals by the magic that surrounds them. I'm not even like Shayna. Since her mate's werewolf essence began residing inside her, she's learned to differentiate *weres* by instinct.

I do well enough, reaching out with my gift to discern the inner beasts lurking within them. The density of their musculature and the way they move and command their stances are very telling. Each characteristic mimics their animal counterparts. I've met many *weres* across the globe and have studied their traits closely. I'm certain I pegged them correctly. The others who appear, though, don't give me the time I need to distinguish them, and their collective power caution that now is not the time.

Weres ease out from their homes, joining those lingering along the stairwell. Some are male, most are female. They watch me closely, trying to pin what and who I am.

My sisters and I are different from any race of human or supernatural on earth. According to our wolves, we give off unique magical aromas that place humans and preternaturals on guard. While I understand, I don't enjoy the attention.

I adjust my purse against my side and walk forward with my head high, feigning confidence I wish came naturally instead of merely skimming the surface of my ivory skin. The purse was a new purchase to go with my blouse and skirt, efforts to look nice for someone I believed was decent.

Ted fooled me. We had dinner just a few blocks away, our conversation was pleasant and polite. There was no flirting and absolutely no sparks. I was sure we'd call it an early night so, his suggestion caught me by surprise. "Will you join me for a drive along the lake, chérie?" he asked. "It's the perfect night to take in the moon and sky."

I agreed and didn't give much thought when he told me we had to return to his apartment to fetch his keys.

There were no keys. No drive. No sky. Only nakedness and more sex organs than anyone should ever need.

"Hey, baby." The cougar steps into my path, the silky way he moves mesmerizing. This isn't someone who sleeps alone much. "Now that your done with that fool Ted, let a real man show you a good time."

I start to tell him no, when the bear interrupts. He mashes out the cigarette on the sole of his ratty sneakers and pulls the cougar back by the arm. "Don't go there," he tells the cougar. "That there is Aric Connor's fam."

I don't see well in the dark. Not like Celia and the wolves do. But I do notice the cougar blanche.

He edges away with his hands up. "Sorry, uh, ma'am, I mean, miss. I didn't mean any disrespect."

"It's all right," I say. My chin trails down as I walk past them, only to snap up when that dark presence returns.

The *weres* growl in that way they do before something meets a gruesome and vomit-inducing death. I can't see their faces with their backs to me, but I recognize they're seconds from charging. The muscles lining their broad shoulders clench and their knees bend. They'll pounce and maul whatever is out here and anything that gets in their way.

A few feet down where the T.V. casts light against the window, another *were* throws open his door and steps out. I can't tell what he is, not from this distance. He's small, closer to my five-foot frame than the behemoths directly in front of me. A honey badger maybe?

"Did ya hear that?" he asks. His growl is lighter and more like a whine but just as fierce.

"Yeah, we did," the bear replies. He takes a strong whiff. "Fuck if it don't smell like shit."

I didn't hear what they did or catch the smell that alerted them. I adjust my hold on the purse straps and inch forward. The cougar's arm shoots out, warning me to stay put. "Get going, little one, before you get hurt. We'll handle this mess."

"I-I can help," I stammer. My voice reflects my raw mood. The experience with Ted eviscerated my heartstrings, and this thing, whatever it is, hasn't helped me settle. So instead of adding backbone to my words, my shaky voice validates the cougar's perceptions that I'm weak.

"Go, little one," the bear insists. "We don't want trouble from the alpha if you bleed."

"I can heal myself," I start to explain.

If they hear me, they don't show it. As a pack, they move as one, picking up their pace when that presence takes off in a sprint. The *weres* who remain perk up, eager to back their brethren. Several swing down from the stairwell overhead and jet after the cougar and bear, while more above race forward, their swift and collective steps barely perceptible.

The *weres* are quick to join the hunt.

And so am I.

Chapter Two

Emme

My feet can't move fast in the sparkly kitten-heels I'm wearing. I do my best and hurry in the opposite direction the *weres* vanished. Bad guys tend to double back to ambush the unsuspecting and the weak. If this thing is one of them, I don't want it to encounter a human. It's strong and dangerous enough to rile the *weres*...although it had no effect on Ted.

I push forward to keep from slowing my pace. Ted didn't sense this thing at all. He should have. His inner animal is akin to other predators. Yet there he stood, his only thoughts on his own desires.

As I reach the next landing, I grab the metal railing to keep my balance. Now is not the time to think of Ted. Danger is afoot and I'm this evening's token Sherlock.

I reach the ground level and rush through the small courtyard that leads out to the street. Two families are barbecuing. The aroma of charred meat fills the small enclosure. Along the grass, their children wrestle and roll around, the youngest ones chasing each other and laughing. Were Alley: this is what this section of North Tahoe is called.

The females bring platters of steaming appetizers to the table, watching me with narrowed gazes. A male eases away from the grill and takes position directly in front of them.

Their wariness reminds me to mind my supernatural manners. With their young so close, the parents will be more combative and quicker to act. My steps slow. I don't want them to think I'll hurt their babies, especially as they've already identified me as a being of magic.

"Good evening," I say. I'm trying to come across friendly, but the tension that licks the air results in me stuttering.

The male grilling steaks abandons his task and stalks forward. He murmurs something I don't catch. He must know me or of me. Whatever he tells the group is enough to negate the strain my presence conveyed. The *weres* nod respectfully. I return the nod and walk away. I want them to enjoy their evening and not stress over me.

The children pause their roughhousing as I pass.

"What was she, Mama?" a little one asks.

I don't wait for her mother's response and resume my quick pace. Our reputation as allies to the *were* elite has helped our relationship with other preternaturals. That doesn't mean we're perceived as friends or that we'll ever belong.

My pulse is racing by the time I reach the walkway. The creature, or whatever it was, is gone. So are the *weres*, and Ted.

I step around glass and chunks of wood from Ted's fall and head away from Were Alley. Once more, I'm on my own.

The next few rows of apartments pass in a blur. I should call an Uber and head home. It's just so early. Everyone will be awake and I'm in no mood to share the details of yet another disastrous date. I took an Uber here, wanting to spare Ted from my brothers-in-law's scrutiny. But Ted, he didn't wish to spare me from anything.

My purse swings gently along my side. I adjust it and keep it in front of me as the breeze from Lake Tahoe picks up.

It's unusually quiet in Were Alley. The loudest sound this evening was likely Ted's vault through the window and his perilous landing several floors below. Brawls are common among *weres*. It's probably why no one made a fuss. Although I shouldn't give Ted another thought, his words remain fresh and continue to burn.

I was a pity date. That's as much as he told me. A little girl who'd have to do since her striking sister was already taken. My shoulders droop. I'm not ugly, but I'm also not my sister Taran. Her beauty and vocabulary make her larger than life. Everyone notices Taran, and everyone should.

The "little girl" comments, reinforced by the other *weres*, also prick at my brain. Being small in stature doesn't make me insignificant, it does, however, portray me as weak and passive and someone easily victimized. It's why Ted felt so free to tell me what he did.

I shake my head, wishing I could also shake the insults. I want to be that person who others think twice before crossing. Not because of who I know. But who I am.

I lift a crumpled piece of paper from the sidewalk and toss it into the trash. No sooner do I step away from it than I fumble for the small container of hand sanitizer in my purse. The moment I flip open the cap and the floral scent reaches my nose, I pause. I frequently stop to rid the world of litter and carry hand sanitizer that comes in pretty aromas. Is it a wonder no one trembles in fear of me?

With that epiphany, I push forward, trying to also to push the self-criticism aside.

Through the last block of Were Alley, streetlamps cast brilliant light and bleach the walkways. Beyond the light waits an inky night absent of stars. If it weren't for the full moon, there would simply be blackness, and the circumspection I've come to know as a friend.

Night hasn't been simply night in a long time. Like a famished animal, it prowls the region, anxious to feast once it's shoved away the sun.

And speaking of entities who love to feast...Oh, Misha. Why did I have to try your BYTEME app?

I thought my perky sister Shayna was pulling my leg when she told me that the local master vampire had developed a dating app for supernaturals. It makes sense with so many members of the mystical community in the area, and from what I hear, it's grown his already massive fortune.

Dating humans is dangerous for beings of magic, more especially for the humans. Despite my apprehensions, I tried it, following more than a little encouragement from my sisters.

"Dude, you have to put yourself out there," Shayna told me.

"No, shit," Taran agreed. "You want to die a miserable old wench like Mancuso over there?" she asked, hooking a thumb in our neighbor's direction.

Like a very irate deer, Mrs. Mancuso popped out of the bushes, wielding two very stiff middle fingers instead of antlers.

As I mentioned, I gave it a go and, well, here I am.

My phone rings. I know it's Shayna long before the image of her grinning face appears. Her upbeat personality perpetually shines through.

"How's it going?" she sings.

Shayna always speaks with gusto. I wish I had that much gusto. Goodness, right now, I'd settle with a dash of perk. "We went back to his place," I admit.

"You did?" Shayna asks. Her voice loses its cheer as she picks up on my lack of enthusiasm.

"Yes. He wanted to fetch his keys so he could take us on a nice, romantic drive along Lake Tahoe."

Shayna sighs. "There weren't any keys, were there, dude?"

"No, but there were plenty of testicles," My blush stings my cheeks. "We went from a nice dinner to him standing naked in front of me."

"Mm. I take it that's when he whipped out the one more than required testicles?" Shayna guesses.

"Yes, all three of them."

"Aw, Em. I'm so sorry. The important thing is you tried. Just give me a sec to get my sword and be on my way."

"Shayna, no. You don't have to—"

She, of course, ignores me to speak to her monstrosity of a husband, Koda. "Puppy, I'll be right back...What...To pick up Emme...She went out with some guy with three testicles she found on Misha's dating app... That's right, three...No, I'm not making this up. Why would I make this up...Yes, I'm taking a sword...Well, because he tried to feel up Emme."

The growls that follow are enough to rupture my eardrum.

"Koda, no...*no*...I'll take care of it...Puppy, you stay in bed all sexy like and wait for me." Shayna drops her voice, whispering low into the phone as if Koda can't hear loud and clear. "We were playing Quaker Oat guy meets Naughty Pilgrim. Between you and me, Koda's getting really good at churning butter—"

More growls followed by several bouts of swearing. "Puppy, don't throw your wig on the floor like that. I paid a lot of money for it...Emme *will not* tell everyone about the butter churning, will you, Em?"

"I really won't," I admit.

"See?" Shayna says. "Nothing to worry about."

"Shayna, I already took care of Ted," I assure her.

"What'd you do to him, dude?" she asks. "Wanna make sure it measures up to what the ol' bugger deserves."

"I, ah, sort of threw him out a window," I admit.

"Yeah?"

"Yes," I reply. I step around a puddle, wishing she hadn't called so soon.

"How many stories?"

"Three," I say, remembering.

"One for each teste?" She doesn't wait for me to answer. "Seems only fair."

I cross the street at the walkway and cut left.

"It's okay, Koda," Shayna adds quickly. "Don't get dressed. Emme took care of business and told that guy and his floppy hairy bits what for...What...You didn't need to hear that...Then why'd you go and ask?"

Shayna is preoccupied with Ted's body parts and that's fine with me. I don't want to tell her about what Ted said to me. It would only further upset my family. I also don't mention that presence I briefly experienced. The *weres* in the neighborhood took charge to defend their territory and telling them will only pull them away from the uh, unique evening they planned.

It wasn't that long ago we took on a necromancer and an army of zombies. They can use the rest and private time.

"I can still come getcha," Shayna offers. "We can stop for ice cream on the way back. All the butter churning made me hungry if you know what I mean."

"Yes, and please don't elaborate," I beg.

I lower the volume, embarrassed someone might hear her only to grimace at the multitude of texts Taran sends.

Did you burn that shit up?

You should have burned that shit up.

I would have burned that shit up.

Son of a bitch.

Who does he think he is, waving his junk like flags in the wind?

Hell, he didn't wave those flags in your face, did he?

That's just nasty.

I text back, no, and thank Taran for that rather descriptive visual. I groan and push away a strand of hair away from my face. "Shayna, you told Taran?" I ask.

"Totally," she admits. "Texted her as soon as you told me all the dirty deets, Em." Her voice quiets and grows a little sad. "We still tell each other everything, don't we?"

No. Not anymore.

"Em?" she says.

"Yes, I'm still here," I assure her.

"You want to do me one and go for ice cream together? I could use the calories since Hot Lifeguard Shayna resuscitates Sexy Virgin Werewolf in Red Speedo is up next."

"I'm not ready to go home," I blurt out over Koda's embarrassed snarls.

I round the corner and look down the street. The upscale restaurants have begun to shut down as the bars and clubs come to life. No, I'm not ready to go home.

Just as I'm not ready to spend the night alone.

Chapter Three

Emme

My phone slides nicely into its designated pocket. Shayna wanted to come for me. Mercifully she didn't press. She realized I needed time away from the house.

Out of all my sisters, I'm closest to Shayna. As hard as she tries though, it's difficult for her to relate to what I'm going through. She doesn't have to trudge through the muddy waters of dating. I do, and my flowery galoshes continue to stick to the gross floor.

My mind wanders, picking through the shift of events. The evening spun from nice to nightmarish as quickly as a top. If I didn't possess the power I do, I would have walked away a victim. Ted would have moved on to the next female he felt worthy of his presence and attempted to wow her with his juggling expertise. He wouldn't have given me another thought. Now, he will, and perhaps think twice about mistreating another female. Oh, and that sinister presence, whatever it was, could have harmed me. I never would have thought to go after something so vile if my abilities couldn't fend off an enemy.

I wince when a pang of pain reminds me there's still healing to perform and magic to call upon. I lift my right hand, my expression softening as pale-yellow light forms on my palm and spreads along my fingertips, soothing away the residual ache from slapping Ted.

I surprised myself by striking him. Violence and aggression aren't attributes I possess. Please don't misunderstand, I've killed in defense of myself and others, but doing so hasn't assuaged me from guilt. Despite my gentle touch, there's blood on my hands, and all the good I've done won't wash the stains from my skin or mind.

"Don't do this to yourself," I whisper.

I shake out my hand as well as the remorse that haunts my dreams. I need to focus on the present if I'm ever to have a future, and if I'm to help protect Celia.

Celia. My oldest sister and my hero. She and Aric are expecting their first child. Of course, like with everything life has given us, there is nothing simple about her pregnancy. The baby she carries is prophesized to save the world from an uprising and evil. That's a startling expectation to aspire to. Poor baby. And poor Celia.

After months of worrying whether her baby was growing, the little bundle of joy grew in a magical burst. Celia went from a barely-there baby bump, to really showing. It was beautiful and frightening all at once.

As if on cue, my phone buzzes, and a text from Celia appears.

Hey, sweetie. Shayna just texted me and told me what happened. Aric isn't familiar with this wolf, but he will be and so will I.

I crinkle my nose. If Ted is a member of Aric's pack, he'll be dealt with and it won't be pretty. If Celia finds him first, it will be worse. Pregnant or not, Celia is scary.

No need, Celia. And please don't think about returning home. Enjoy your weekend with Aric. Please. I'm safe and I'll be all right.

The extra please is necessary and what it takes for her to agree to let it go, at least for now. The part about being all right isn't exactly true. But I will be.

I return my phone to its pocket and continue my walk. The breeze from the lake bats at my white flowy skirt. I shudder, although it's not from the magic the lake carries. Celia was always sensitive to the lake's magic. Me, I'm just cold.

It's cooler for July than I'm accustomed to and my sleeveless dress exposes my arms. I would have brought a sweater had I known the evening would mimic fall instead of summer. I glance over my shoulder when something pokes at my senses, alerting me that it's not just the temperature causing me to tremble.

Well-kept walkways that lead to small boutiques and casual bistros stretch out the length of the block. As far as company, I remain the only guest at the party. I maneuver around another puddle. My feet barely reach the other side when I quickly turn, expecting to find someone lurking close by.

There aren't footsteps or voices, just a presence. I stop, waiting for someone, anyone, to appear; a shop owner locking up for the night or a resident skipping out of her apartment to take advantage of her youth and the nightlife.

There's nothing. But something all at once.

It's a different sensation than what I felt at Ted's apartment. There's no fear alerting me to run or that primal warning that screams of danger. Whatever I feel isn't evil or hateful. It simply is.

I glance back more than once. Tahoe isn't generally considered a largely ghost-inhabited region. There are certainly hot spots for paranormal activity and wandering spirits have a way of making their presence known. But a spirit isn't what I feel. It takes another block and a few more cautious steps before the feeling of being tracked lessens and ultimately fades away.

Rain had come and gone earlier this afternoon. The remains of the steady showers that threatened to turn into storms only apparent in the moist air and along the small pools of water reflecting the full moon's dull white rays.

Ahead of me, a couple crosses the street holding hands and speaking quietly. Their night only just began. Mine may come to an abrupt close if I don't find who I'm searching for.

There are single women in my position who would give up after an experience like I had with Ted. They'd call it a night and go home. I can't blame them. Not long ago, I would have, too. I'd have taken Shayna up on her offer for ice cream and returned home, binged watched Netflix alone while she churned butter with Koda.

Except home doesn't feel like home anymore. It hasn't for a long, long time.

Through their ups and downs and terrifying ordeals, my sisters found their mates. Or maybe it's better to say, their mates found them.

Mate. I initially shied away from that term. It sounds sexual and primordial, more lust than love. It wasn't until we met the *weres* that I realized how sacred and precious the word is.

It's magical. A love so deep and binding, one mate typically can't survive without the other. I was always a fan of love. Lust, not so much. I'm not a virgin. I'm just experienced enough to recognize love is forever and lust doesn't last.

Seeing how my sisters are with their mates, it's my constant desire to have one too, or at least someone close to that. I suppose that's why home has lost its comfort. My sisters and their wolves are so connected, so *bonded*, I'm more of an outsider looking in instead of a family member who belongs with her pack.

A car speeds by me, blasting Cardi B and muffling the excited chatter of the passengers. I try to smile in their direction and be happy for them. I don't quite manage.

Smiles don't come easy anymore, except when I'm around that one werewolf I know. Perhaps it's because like me, Bren knows what it's like to be alone.

Goodness. I wish I wasn't so depressed and that every year that passes would lighten my mood instead of worsening it. It's more than the loneliness I feel to not have someone special in my life, and it's more than losing Liam, although I miss him and think of him often. It's everything.

Liam was my friend and lover until he wasn't. Until he found the mate I never was to him. We were close and passionate. He was sweet and strong and doting. I was convinced there was no one better. He was the man I pictured marrying and sharing forever with. But despite our strong connection, it paled in comparison to what he found in Allie.

The way Ted spoke of Liam was disrespectful to such a good man and hero among *weres*. But it was also an insult to him and Allie. Out of respect for their memory, I wouldn't stand for it.

I will always love Liam. And I will always protect him and the female who won his heart. They deserve as much.

Hopefully, I do, too.

As I reach the next block, the entire neighborhood comes alive, a harsh reminder that life continues forward even if you want it to pause. Music and laughter reverberate from all sides. Crowds of twenty and thirty somethings line the streets at the more popular and exclusive clubs. I used to enjoy those types of clubs. Tonight, I desire something much different.

The Watering Hole is the one bar in North Tahoe *weres* frequent the most. It overlooks the lake and always draws a decent crowd of supernaturals. The lake's magic is so pure, it is considered among the most pre-emptive sources of magic on earth. It's why so many mystical beings are drawn to it. It's sad humans can't experience such a pure power like Tahoe possesses, but it seems I share that sentiment alone.

"Humans would just fuck up the lake, like they did when only Native American werebeasts inhabited the region," Koda once told me.

I suppose he's right. Humans do have a way of tainting the world.

My pace quickens when the bright blue neon sign of the Watering Hole comes into view. Originally more club than bar, patrons now prefer drinking and socializing on the dance floor to grinding and twerking. I don't grind or twerk, ever, and I'm not much of a drinker. But after my night, I need a smile.

And no one makes me smile like Bren.

Despite being part of the pack, Bren bartends at the Watering Hole. After years of being a *lone* werewolf, he continues to connect better with random strangers than his fellow *weres*. I understand. For years, my sisters and I, along with his roommate, Danny, were his pack. Now, I'm not certain what we are.

Bren used to be so affectionate. That changed on our last adventure. He didn't want me anywhere near him and seemed afraid to touch me. Or better said, he was afraid to have me touch him.

We were badly beat up, and I only meant to help him heal. Bren, being Bren, wanted me to save my energy and tend to myself. Or so he said.

I smooth out my fluttery gossamer skirt. It goes nicely with my shimmering scoop-neck top. My attire was meant for a nice dinner and is very unlike the scantily and outrageous outfits the ladies waiting across the street have squeezed into.

As I observe their daring, selfie-taking techniques, I'm very glad Bren bartends at the Hole, where there's less noise and where it's slightly more conservative. It's the atmosphere I need and exactly what will distract me from my negative thoughts. I take my place in line, my heartbeat steadily increasing the closer I draw to the entrance.

The vampire playing bouncer at the door allows four women through without incident. He must be new to the family. It would explain why he's here and not frolicking through Misha's estate with the rest of the clan.

The girls ahead of me fall all over themselves gawking at the bouncer. Vampires have that way of turning humans on, and while they're gorgeous, the vampire doesn't give them much thought. He must have had his fill of blood for the moment.

I ease forward, ready to pay my admission fee until he slides off his stool and blocks me.

"Sorry, kid. You have to be twenty-one to get in."

"Um. I realize that, um, sir."

A blush finds its way to my cheeks. I dig for my wallet and produce three forms of ID.

He angles his eyebrows like I'm trying to deceive him and flips through my identification. "Emme Wird." he says slowly. "I know you. You're one of the ones the master told us to watch out for."

"Ah, yes. Misha is rather protective of us," I stammer.

"*Misha?*" he asks.

Oh, and there's another blush. The bouncer is stunned I didn't refer to Misha as Master Aleksandr or something equally as formal. And because of it, he grasps just how friendly we are with the most powerful vampire on earth.

Yet, it's my appearance he fixates on.

"Shit," he says. "You're twenty-three? You barely look legal."

I frown and steel myself for another "little girl" remark.

Like most, he doesn't exactly tremble in fear at my scowl.

"You're cute," he says, flashing some fang. "I get off at two. Wait for me. I'll take you out and show you a good time."

Heat pushes its way from my face to my neck, enticing the vampire to latch his attention to my jugular. "Um. No, thank you."

He leans back on his heels and crosses his arms, appearing amused. "Did you just say no thank you?"

Long dark waves of blue-black hair frame flawless, deep olive skin and gray eyes, that women would pay to ogle at, sparkle back at me. This vampire is not used to hearing no.

"Ah, yes?" I offer.

"I don't think you understand. With me, you're guaranteed a good time."

I start to explain that our last good time with an undead landed us in Vampire Court. His interest drifts from me and toward the direction I arrived from. His gaze narrows as if in a standoff with another predator. When I glance behind me and find nothing, I use the opportunity to slip inside, stopping suddenly when the vampire furrows his brow into a menacing scowl.

Another vampire appears, whispering something that makes the bouncer laugh. He eases back down to his stool, maintaining his focus further down the street.

My pace isn't as quick as it was, naturally slowing from the unusual encounter. It's a good thing. I don't want to appear anxious. Except now that I'm here, it's an emotion I can't suppress.

A Chris Young tribute band blasts away, replacing the regular DJ and the equipment she uses. The lead singer is good, belting out *Raised on Country* and making it his own.

The crowd trickles onto the dance floor and closer to the band, the hoots and hollers growing in numbers as more take to the floor.

The space isn't cluttered, and I easily snake my way through. I love it. Being petite and thin, it doesn't take large numbers to trample me. Too many times I've relied on my sisters or used my *force* to avoid being knocked to the ground.

The smile I couldn't muster before easily appears when I find Bren working the rear bar. He fills a pitcher with beer while pouring whiskey for two men. With a flick of his elbow, he turns off the tap and tops off the glasses filled with ice.

A charcoal gray and navy flannel shirt stretches across his broad shoulders, years of wear threatening to rip the fabric with just one good flex. It's the one Celia bought him the first Christmas we celebrated together. It lightens those eyes that I swear shed tears when he opened his gift. He loved that we thought enough of him to buy him gifts and include him in our celebration.

Mostly, he just loved us.

I place my purse on the hook beneath the bar and take a seat at the corner. He's working hard and I don't want to disrupt his flow. I twist slightly to scan the area. For the moment, there aren't any girls flirting with Bren. That will change. For now, he's mine.

Well, I don't mean *mine*.

At least, not yet...

Chapter Four

Emme

Thoughts of Bren being mine, for even one night, cues my next blush. The first time I was attracted to Bren was the first time we met and he, well, *breathed*. He thought of me as a "kid" and laughed when I asked him for a date. It's a good thing I don't embarrass easily, says the person who embarrasses *very* easily.

Bren scratches his light beard. It's slightly darker than his wavy brown hair, and something he usually does when he's agitated or thinking matters through. He tilts his head as he reaches for a bottle of scotch. The motion is brief, just enough for me to catch a glimpse at his eyes. They're deep blue, not the typical werewolf brown or amber.

He must have inherited those pretty eyes from his human mother. I'd ask him, but Bren is very closed-mouthed about his life as a *lone* and extremely private when it comes to his parents. There's a lot we don't know about his past, just enough to see that he's suffered his lion's share of pain.

I pass my fingers along the slick wood, realizing how much I'm crushing on Bren. I've ignored my feelings for a while, certain his feelings for me had not changed until our latest supernatural debacle. We were hurt. Blood and soil soaked our skin and hair and my clothes clung to me in tatters. I thought I saw him looking at me *that way*, the way that demonstrated how much I've changed and how the challenges we've endured these past few years have matured me well beyond my years. Maybe I imagined it. Maybe it was nothing. Like Taran used to say, "Just cause you're looking doesn't mean you want to ride that cowboy bareback till sunrise."

I wince. Okay, perhaps that wasn't the greatest Taran quote I could have referenced.

Bren slaps his hand down on a tip and pockets it. "Much appreciated," he tells the man who left it.

He catches my aroma and whips his head in my direction. "Hey," he says, surprise marching across his features like an army. "I didn't see you there."

His words are staggered, reflecting the shock my presence evidently stirred. "Hi, Bren," I say. I offer a small wave. Even though mere feet separate us, he feels so far away. "I just sat down. I didn't mean to distract you."

If all those years hadn't passed, and the wolves remained strangers to us, I would have sat closer. I'd kiss Bren hello and instantly start talking to him. He'd jabber on about his day or say something loud and inappropriate that would leave me covering my face and no-doubt in stitches. It's the way things used to be for us.

My sisters still hug him, even though it sets off their wolves. I don't have anyone and I can't get anywhere near him.

Bren has kept his distance from me and there are moments when he's wrenched away to avoid my touch. Those moments were tense, and danger surrounded us like a swarm of murder hornets, so I tried to understand. But there's no tension today, and most especially, no danger, right?

His features relax, along with his typically booming voice. "Hey, sweet thing," he says. "Slide on over and keep me company."

The grin he pegs me with completely changes his expression from the werewolf wary mask he habitually wears to that of the charming and friendly guy I once knew so well.

He reaches for a glass over his head, causing the front of his flannel shirt to open. A black T-shirt is not so neatly tucked beneath his favorite pair of old jeans, and I'll bet he's wearing his most beaten-up pair of work boots. He dresses for comfort and doesn't care what others think. It's one of many things that make him Bren.

My purse is barely in its new spot when he places his forearms on the bar. "Nice dress," he says.

"Thank you. It's actually a blouse and top." I lower myself to the stool. I probably shouldn't lean in too close. I don't want to send Bren running like I have in the past, yet the loneliness that's troubled me for months keeps me in place.

When he doesn't withdraw, I edge closer, allowing the intimacy and kindness I seek. The warmth his body stirs elates and feeds my starving soul. I need Bren. God, I really do.

"Are they new?" he asks when I say nothing more.

I don't mean to lose myself in the moment, yet I do. "My attire?" I ask, hesitantly.

Bren chuckles. "Yeah. What else would I be asking about?"

My nose crinkles and I find myself growing shy. "Maybe my purse, too?" I offer.

"Now you're pushing it, Em."

I laugh. "Yes, my clothes are new, Bren."

It's nice of him to notice, no, to *be noticed*. I picked out these items on sale. They're comfortable and stylish and I immediately loved them. I love them more now because Bren saw me in them.

"Thank you for noticing," I add quietly.

He cocks an eyebrow. "That you look nice?"

"Yes," I say. "It means a lot."

His humor fades at my softening features. "Well, don't get too excited, princess. Danny's manners might just be finally rubbing off on me."

Bren's former roommate spends more time at the Den than anywhere else. He texted me a few days ago to ask how we were. Even though we had a nice conversation, as Bren begins to edge away, I ask more about Danny to keep Bren in place.

"How is Danny? It's been a while since I've seen him."

Bren rolls his eyes and lifts a ticket the waitress drops in front of him. "He's horny, Emme. That's how he is. He and Heidi are doing it like fly-ing monkeys on the Wicked Witch's broom during a tornado."

I didn't need that visual. But there it is and no, it's not going any-where. "I'm not sure that makes sense," I reply.

He tucks the ticket between his two fingers and points at me. "Nope. But that's some funny shit right there."

I grin, unable to help myself. "Of course, it is," I reply.

Another waitress appears and slams her empty tray in front of him. "Damn metrosexuals," she mutters. "When did men stop dressing like real men?"

She gives Bren the once-over. I don't think he notices. Bren glances at me, holding tight to his smirk and pours a round of shots. Unlike the sly smiles he flashes other women, the ones he directs at me are genuine and reach his eyes. For that, and more, I'm grateful.

As quickly as he places the shots on the tray, the waitress flounces away with it, appearing annoyed. Bren doesn't bother with her. He wipes off the counter and pours me a glass of white wine. "Harvest Riesling, right?"

My favorite wine. "You remembered," I say. "Thank you."

I take a chance and lift off the stool to kiss his cheek. My clumsiness gets in the way and I knock over the wineglass.

Bren turns quickly to make a grab for it.

And my lips accidently graze his.

Shock mars Bren's features. Slowly, he places the glass back on the bar.

He's dumbstruck. I am, too. Everything happened so quickly, hardly any wine splashed across the bar.

Our kiss was barely there. Brief. *Sweet.* Yet hot enough to scorch my legs.

I force my toes to uncurl and glance around awkwardly when he just stares.

"Ah. Sorry," I offer. "I meant to aim for your cheek."

He straightens. "You sayin' you wanted to take the glass, *that glass—*" He points. –"And smash it against my face?"

Humiliation throws me into panic and awkward mode. "No, *no.* The kiss. Kissing you. I meant to kiss your cheek. The one on your face," I add like an imbecile.

I cover my eyes. This is one of the many reasons I tend to stay quiet. Speaking hasn't worked out for me much.

Bren's releases a heavy sigh and swipes at this face. "Thanks for clearing that up." He winks. "I was sure you wanted to cut my face and kiss my ass."

Bren throws his head back and laughs when I gape at him. "Em, relax. I'm just messing with you."

"I am sorry," I stammer, wishing my reply didn't sound so high-pitched.

Bren wraps his hand around the base of my neck and pulls me to him. His lips soft and warm against my forehead. "Don't be," he whispers. "I've waited years for that kiss."

The clouds break and the world erupts with sunshine. "Really?" I ask. The excitement in my voice gives us pause. Once more, I wish my power included turning back time.

Bren analyzes me closely and takes a deep breath, using his heightened sense to determine if I'm lying or if I'm seriously that much of a simpleton. Had I my sisters' olive complexion, my blushes wouldn't be so obvious. Except I don't, and here I am, again.

Bren edges away from me. "I'll pour you another glass," he says carefully, his watchful gaze hitched on me.

"I'll just have water please." I play nervously with my hands. My exchange with Bren has been juvenile at best. Alcohol won't make me more prolific.

Bren pours me a water and places it in front of me. "Thank you," I mumble, hoping my skin has returned to a less mortified shade of red.

He greets me with a tender smile. It's all I seem to need. Relief washes over me. Maybe things between us aren't so bad after all. Maybe, we're going to be all right.

The waitress from before returns, interrupting by slapping her tray on the bar and waving the ticket at Bren, her annoyance having doubled since she last appeared.

Bren pushes away from the bar. "Give me a sec, okay?" he says.

I nod and turn my attention toward the waitress when she huffs. She's ready to snap someone in two. She's human, and unbeknownst to her, surrounded by beasts known to exude their dominance. Her job can't be easy.

"Are you okay?" I ask.

The scowl she greets me with suggests I shouldn't have asked and why don't I just run along and burn in hell.

She huffs again and gives me her back, adjusting the fastener holding her ruby red hair in place. "Bren," she says. "What are you doing? Did you forget how to read? The assholes at table eight only want top shelf. My tip depends on it, baby."

I stiffen at the "baby" reference. It's not that she said it, it's how she said it. If I know Bren, they're more than just coworkers.

"Sorry, Nance," Bren mutters. "I'm on it."

"Lai-la," she enunciates.

"What?" Bren says, looking up.

"Nancy quit two years ago, dipshit. I'm Laila."

Bren pours vodka into a mixer and gives it a few shakes. "Hmph? No kidding. I really liked her."

Oh, and doesn't that make Laila mad? Yet somehow, I'm the one she trains her steely features on.

I adjust my position and try to relax despite her irate state. I'm having trouble keeping my eyes off Bren and based on another loathsome glare from Laila, she's noticed.

Bren is just being Bren. He's dressed as casually as ever and he's wearing clothes I've seen him wear a thousand times before. But...he looks really cute tonight. Very much a younger, leaner version of Blake Shelton like Shayna once described.

"What's wrong, Emme?"

I jolt at his voice. I'm so caught up in trying not to look at him that I didn't see him approach. I clear my throat as the band transitions to Sam Hunt's *Hard to Forget*.

"Sorry?"

He rubs his beard, scrutinizing me closely. "I asked you why you're by yourself."

"Celia is away for the weekend," I begin. "After what happened with the zombies, Aric thought she was due for some peace, quiet, and less mutilation. He arranged a romantic getaway with plans to return by Monday." I lower my chin, hoping he doesn't ask me too much about my sisters. "Shayna is with Koda."

Bren holds out his hands. "Let me guess, Zorro meets shy, virgin, Mexican villager, and Koda ripped the skirt getting it on?"

That was two weeks ago and no, that skirt never stood a chance against Koda's magnificent glutes, I obviously don't say. I clear my throat, trying to remain elusive. "They're having some time alone at the house, yes."

"I'll bet." Bren crosses his arms, freezing when I shrink inward. "Emme, what aren't you telling me?"

"Nothing."

"Quit lying." He rubs his jaw, his smirk growing ever so knowingly. "Where's Taran?"

I play with the straw in my water as if it's my first time using one. He had to go and ask about the one sister I don't want to talk about. "Taran?" I ask. "Did you say Taran?"

"Yeah, Taran." He leans back on his heels. "Em, where is she?"

I find somewhere else to look. "You know Taran. She's always busy."

"Uh, huh. And what is she busy doing?"

I rub my hands as if there's something on them. "Working," I say.

"At the hospital?" he presses.

There's no point in lying. I'm not good at it and heaven knows Bren can sniff through every word coming out of my mouth. "She's doing something for Misha."

"Misha," Bren says, practically spitting on the ground. "Taran is working for *Misha*?"

Bren has as much love for our resident master vampire as the rest of the *weres*. "Yes."

"And Gemini allowed it?" Bren asks. He's not really asking, he's telling me that there's no way her mate is on board with Team Misha, and he's right.

"I think 'allowed' is too strong a word," I admit. I crinkle my nose, remembering the way Gemini lost his mind when he found out. His twin wolf shot out of his back and snapped the kitchen table in half.

Bren chuckles. "Aw, man. Taran didn't tell Gemini she was working for Misha, did she?"

"Um," is all I say.

Bren shakes his head. "Let me guess, Shayna sang like a canary, didn't she?"

"Ah," I reply. See? This is why I don't talk much.

His smile turns slick. "Kind of like you're about to do. Right now. To me. Start singing."

My mouth opens slightly. "I will not."

Bren leans forward. "So, you do know? What's she's doing for Misha? And what the hell trouble is she in this time?"

I tried to be a spy once. I had a disguise and a mission and everything. We refer to it as "the incident" and no one is allowed to discuss it in my presence.

"Well?" Bren pushes.

"I...I need tampons," I blurt out.

"Huh?"

"Tampons?' I repeat.

I don't really need tampons. My cycle finished last week. It's just a distraction tactic Taran came up with to avoid coming clean with the males in our lives when we're involved in something they wouldn't approve of and will likely get us arrested and / or killed—for the greater good, always. Well, almost always for the greater good.

For some reason, it really works.

"Tampons?" he clarifies.

I don't get the chance to respond. He holds up his hands and backs away, more than proving that no matter how sordid, there's always something to Taran's logic.

"Can't help you there, babe," Bren tells me. He watches me sip my water. It's then his features change. "Are you...are you meeting someone here?"

There's a light snarl to his voice, almost imperceptible, but definitely there. I play with my hair, wondering what he's thinking and why he appears so bothered.

I would never bring a date here, and the only male I've brought around Bren was Liam. Something about another man, especially a *were* in Bren's presence seems wrong, a betrayal I can't explain.

Bren's focus travels from my hand and to my face.

My hand falls away from my hair and still he doesn't move.

There's no reason to keep my night a secret and promptly explain. "I was on a date, earlier, but I didn't have a good time."

His voice lowers. "Why not?"

Bren doesn't bother to mask the irritation in his voice. As part of his chosen pack, he was always protective. "The wolf, Ted, wasn't who I thought he was."

"Those assholes you waste your time on never are, Emme," Bren says. He snags another ticket and pops open several bottles of beer, his motions usually smooth and well-learned, are now aggressive.

I don't discuss my social life with Bren. It's odd that he knows how awful my dating history is. I speak carefully, not wanting to upset him further. "I haven't had much luck," I admit. "But I'm trying. I...I don't want to be alone."

The truth spills out of me without my permission. I didn't want it to, especially in front of Bren, but here it is, mingling with the band's increasing tempo and the aroma of cologne and freshly poured beer.

Bren stills with the beer in his hand, the top already popped and lying somewhere on the floor. He swallows hard. "Did he...touch you, kiss you, shit like that?"

His question stiffens my spine. Is he really going there? "No," I admit.

He sighs, relieved. "Good."

I make a face. "He was too busy stripping out of his clothes and asking if I liked what I saw."

"On the street?" Bren asks.

"No, *no*. In his apartment over on Were Alley."

Bren slams the beer on the bar, shattering it. "Fuck," he snarls.

He sticks his hand into an empty bucket and shakes off the shards of glass imbedded into his skin. With another snarl, he wipes up the mess with a rag.

Like all *weres*, Bren's skin tough. The glass doesn't appear to have punctured deep enough to cut. Still, I reach for his palm, bent on inspecting it for damage.

He pulls away. "Why the hell did you follow some asshole back to his apartment?" he demands.

Bren's reply and anger take me aback. "Why do you think?"

I hold out a hand when his eyes fly open. "I don't mean it that way. What I'm saying is, we were on a date and that's something people on dates often do."

I shut my mouth when I realize how many loitering *weres* are listening in on my latest debacle. The band has pulled in a larger crowd from the street. Most are human. Those closest to the bar are *weres* and they look familiar.

"Ted offered to take me for a ride along the lake," I say, lowering my voice. "He said he'd left his keys in his apartment."

"Emme, the only place he wanted to take you was to bed," Bren tells me flatly. "No one takes romantic drives anymore. It's just shit he made up to get you back to his place."

"I realize that now," I reply.

"The idiot probably doesn't even own a car," he adds.

My shoulders droop when the *weres* behind me laugh. I only hope they're not laughing at me. "I get it, Bren," I whisper. "You don't have rub it in."

He groans and swipes his face when I shrink further inward. "I'm not trying to make you feel worse. There're just a lot of horny bastards out there. And some of these newbies trying to get into the pack aren't disciplined at all, you feel me? The war took out a lot of the strong, traditional alphas, the goody-goody-types who fiercely instilled right from wrong. At best, these morons have learned not to munch on humans, at worst..." He motions to me with an irritated gesture. "You get Donald."

"Ted," I clarify.

"Whatever," he mutters. "Still an asshole."

I lift my glass to take another sip of water. The rim doesn't quite reach my lips when I return it to the bar.

"What's wrong?" Bren asks.

The stress of how really bad the night was hits me all at once and I haven't even told him about the presence I felt and all the *weres* who went after it. "Ted wasn't disciplined, like you said," I admit. "He wasn't careful with me or his words."

Bren doesn't move. "You saying he hurt you?"

Yes. He did. But I wish I hadn't let him.

"Not in the physical sense," I reply. I play with the glass in my hand. "He said things about me and about Liam and his mate. He told me it was actually Taran he wanted and only went out with me because I was available and he felt sorry for me."

"What the hell?" Bren says, no longer trying be quiet. "I'll kick his ass."

Bren places his palm on the bar, ready to leap over and track Ted down. I grasp his wrist, my touch nothing compared to his brute strength, but enough to keep him in place. "It's all right," I tell him. "I made it clear he was out of line when I threw him out the window—"

Bren regards me as is if he doesn't recognize me. "You threw him out the window?"

"Yes?" I say.

Bren leans in and smiles with enough warmth to melt the ice cubes in my glass. The annoyance darkening his features skitters away, leaving only the wolf I know and adore.

"That's my girl," he says, skimming his rough knuckles against my cheek.

A tease of heat flickers along my skin with Bren's caress, stirring desire and invigorating my tormented spirit. I welcome the ardor like my next breath, claiming it and permitting it to lick the scars marring my damaged soul.

Bren stops, his eyes widening as if he's committing the most heinous sin. Pain, anger, greed, and rapture—every emotion akin to grief warring along his features.

"Bren," I whisper, sensing him pull away.

He doesn't want me. He's withdrawing, abandoning me and my touch, just as he's done before.

But then, he doesn't, returning like an unbridled storm.

Bren hooks his arm around my neck and pulls me to him.

He kisses me, savagely, his tongue probing and dominating.
This time, it's not an accident.
This time, we both mean it.
This time, the world vanishes, and Bren and I become one.

Chapter Five

Bren

I wrench myself off Emme. It takes some doing, the cement or whatever invisible glue is pinning me to her making it damn near impossible.

My back smacks against a row of bottles, tipping some over and knocking even more to the floor. My heart is making mincemeat out of my chest. I'm having the big one, I know I am.

What the fuck?

What the actual fuck?

Emme is sweating and panting, her face so red she's a hard second away from passing out.

"Hey," I say, like an absolute moron.

She makes a noise. I think. A word mixed with a sound. Aside from that, she keeps quiet, keeps breathing, keeps sweating.

Shit. I think I killed her with my hotness.

Damn my sexiness to hell.

Seriously, why did I do that? Why did I kiss her?

Because you've wanted to for a long time now, asshole.

"Yo, dude." A werewolf in a houndstooth jacket motions me over. Who the hell wears houndstooth to the Hole? He plannin' on going pheasant hunting up in this bitch?

I point to him but speak to Emme. "I'll be right back, okay?"

"Unt," she says. Or something like that.

Aw, hell. I hope she's still alive when I get back.

My feet feel heavy. I have to practically lift them with my arms. I stop when I see the wolf is accompanied by three more *weres*. All newbies, all dressed like they're on their way to Coachella or whatever the fuck.

"What do you want?" I ask.

"Witch's Brew," the wolf who called me over says. He exchanges glances with his pals. "Word on the street says you got some."

"Word on the street?" I ask, looking at them like they deserve to be looked at. "You mean the mean streets of Tahoe?"

"Ya," he says.

Whatever. I have to get back to Emme. "Sure. Whatever. It's a hundred a bottle. How many do you want?"

Again, they look at each other. For *weres*, none of these idiots feel dominant. They're more like betas or omegas, sure to be mowed over by the seasoned *weres* in Aric's pack.

"Why so much?" the weremongoose in the orange T-shirt polo asks.

I roll my eyes. "Cause it's witch's brew, dumbass. One bottle is all it takes. Do you want to pour human beer down your throat all night and still not get a buzz?"

"Uh, no?"

"Then one hundred for one bottle, bro," I tell him. I take another look at him. He's not really the "bro" type. More like the second cousin twice removed who likes to eat sand when no one's looking.

A smaller wolf eases forward. "You don't understand. We're part of the pack," he says. "Your pack." He points to the first guy. "And he's a pureblood, one of the last few left."

I grin. "Pureblood, huh?" I ask. They nod, expecting me to bow or some shit. I lose my smile. "Then he can afford it."

When they just stare, I push off the bar and throw my hands up in surrender. "If you can't handle the brew or the price, I can whip you boys up some Shirley Temples on the house. After all, you are pack."

The so-called pureblood sighs and whips out his card. "We'll take four," he mumbles.

I take the card and print out the receipt. "Don't forget to leave a tip," I say, giving him a wink.

Before lowering to the floor to unlock the brew safe, I steal a glance at Emme. Her face is still flushed but better. I'm no longer worried she'll keel over from all the manly, male hormones I hit her with when I kissed her.

What the hell's wrong with me? I kissed Emme. *Emme.*

Maybe it's been too long since I got some. Wait, didn't I just bang Sally a few weeks ago? Or was it Jennifer? It couldn't have been that good if I can't remember her name. Maybe that's my problem. I barely have sex anymore, and when I do, it's all about what I can do for them. Word spreads quick when you're hung like a bear instead of a wolf.

The spell the witches cast over the safe takes a moment to recognize me before it clicks open.

"Yo, dude," Houndstooth guy says. "How you coming along with all those brewskies? Your boys are thirsty."

I sigh. I should punch him in the face just for just saying "brewskies." Instead, I take the higher road. "You want the beers?" I ask.

"Yeah," they all say.

"Then shut up," I snap.

See? I can keep it classy.

I reach for the first beer. It glows when I touch it. I don't want the damn bottle to explode in my face and give it a second for it to allow me to take it. That's right, "allow." The witches who made it don't just want anyone to handle their stash. Witches need to get paid.

I pop the cap when the warning it emanates lessens and ease the bottle onto the bar. "Wait," I say when Houndstooth tries to snag it. "This is the real stuff. If you grab it before it's ready for you, you'll be wearing it."

Houndstooth huffs, trying to look tough for his friends and whips the beer off the bar. The brew gets angry and the lot of us end up sprayed.

From across the bar, a werehyena laughs, setting off his friends. "Brew Virgins," he calls out.

I swipe my face with a clean towel, watching as the wolf and his boys lick the trickling beer from their lips. Their eyes widen and their pupils immediately dilate.

"Whoa," Orange Polo says. "This is some good stuff."

"You've never had witch's brew before, have you?" I ask.

Houndstooth goes all red in the face. "No," he admits.

"First lesson," I say. "Respect it and the magic it took to make it."

"Yes, sir," he says. He passes me his card. I pass him a towel to clean up his mess.

I stop in place when I see the hyena make his way to Emme. He offers to buy her a drink. She politely declines, her attention on me. I'm not sure what the hyena catches in my face, but it's enough to send him and his buddies in the direction of the band and away from Emme.

Good boy. Smart boy. Stay away and everyone will keep their limbs.

I bend and reach for the next brew. Emme looks damn sweet tonight. I mean, she always looks sweet, but it's like, everything about her is different. She's a woman, I guess. She grew up in front of me before I was ready.

Okay, that's not right either. Emme was always a woman. A beautiful young woman. If I had a twenty for every guy I've had to keep off of her...Maybe it's that top. It's brown-gold, or gold-brown. Whatever it is, she looks nice in it.

Emme is just, different lately. I can't put my finger on when it happened, she just changed. It might be when we went on that mission (the one we're not allowed to talk about in front of her), and I saw how much that idiot wanted her. No, not wanted her. Wanted to do stuff to her. Wanted to hurt her like only men could hurt women.

It wasn't like that when Emme was with Liam. They were closer in age. He was good to her and for a long time, she was everything to that wolf. It made it okay for them to be together. But then Liam was gone, and Emme went from that kid I would've busted heads for to, *hell*, someone I'd still bust heads for.

The first bottle reaches the Houndstooth without incident and Orange Polo handles the second bottle like it might bite. Good for him. I've seen witch's brew sprout teeth and take off chunks of skin.

I steal another glance at Emme. She's staring hard at her glass. The crowd size has doubled since she arrived and there are more humans now than *weres*. I can't ignore her like I've been. No. Not this time.

Everything about her has totally bloomed. Her skin looks different. Was it always that soft? I don't know. I haven't touched her, and when she's tried to touch me, my wolf warned against it. He shoved us away from her, telling us this thing I'm feeling is wrong.

It is wrong? She's Emme. Emme with those tiny freckles on her face she's so ashamed of. She doesn't get that they add to her cuteness. I wonder where else she has freckles...

Man. Don't go there. You don't shit where you eat. If the old man taught me anything, it was that.

I place the last witch's brew on the bar. "Can I touch it?" Red Polyester shirt asks. He points to it.

My gaze cuts to Emme. "Not without permission."

I'll be fine. Emme will be fine. All I have to do is keep my distance. So long as she doesn't crinkle her nose in that sweet way of hers, we'll all be fine.

Another glance at Emme, another wave of emotions when our eyes lock. Her soft green irises take me in, looking at me like I don't think she ever has. I'd remember it if she stared at me this way before.

I do a double-take when I realize how many people are waiting for drinks. "Keep it together," I mutter.

I manage to pass out two pitchers and am pouring a third round of shots when my phone rings, instantly swearing when I see a full moon flash across the screen. "Mother's ass," I mumble.

"Yeah?" I ask.

"We have a situation," Koda growls into the phone.

My hand lowers when he spills the details. I march to Emme, startling her when she finds me in front of her.

"Emme, what was the wolf's name you went out with tonight?"

She puckers her brow. "Ted Savante. Why?"

"They just found him ripped to pieces."

Chapter Six

Bren

Emme turns a lighter shade of pale. "Ted's...*dead*?" she asks.

"Totally," I say. I lean in, whispering low. "That wasn't you, was it?"

Her jaw pops open. "No."

I hold out a hand. "Because if it was, you could tell me. We've got you, and it's not like Aric won't cover for you."

"Bren, I didn't kill Ted."

"Or rip him to pieces, like, on accident?" I ask.

"No, Bren," she says. "And before you ask, I would remember if I did."

"Good to know," I say.

The werehyena shoves his phone into the back of his jeans and ambles over with his friends. Yeah, they all got the call, too.

"We're told you're in charge," the hyena tells me. "How do you want to handle it?"

I shoot him the best Tom Cruise *Mission Impossible* shit-just-got-real face I can muster. "The only way we know how." I then give them my back and speak low into the phone. "What the hell do you mean I'm in charge?" I growl.

Koda, the baby-ducklings-knitting-booties-over rainbows-guy holds my hand and offers support and encouragement like only he can. "You think I like this any better, asshole? Aric's away. Gemini is in route to

Iran to look for Taran—something about her setting a sacred mountain shrine on fire, and bodies of witches are popping up all over the Nevada side."

"Are you messing with me right now?" I ask. "Didn't we just annihilate a zombie army a few weeks ago?"

"Is this a good time to remind you evil doesn't care, Bren?" Koda barks back. "Genevieve is out-right pissed off. These witches aren't part of her coven, but the head witches the dead belong to are demanding justice since it happened under Genevieve's watch and our territory. It's a political nightmare. Shayna's coming with me to make sure I don't snap someone's broom in half and we can't get a hold of Emme."

My focus drifts back to Emme, and the growing number of *weres* gathered around her. They know she's one of us, except most of them are looking at her like more than just an ally.

"Emme is with me," I growl, at them.

Koda thinks I'm talking to him. "Good. Take her with you. She'll keep your ass out of trouble."

With that, he disconnects and I'm the one in charge.

"Hey," the human in the white shirt yells. "Can we get some service here?"

The glare I peg him with knocks him off his stool, and he like, runs away. I roll my eyes and saunter over to the *weres*, taking control and showing these bitches (except for Emme) how it's done.

"All right, pussies. Which one of you knows how to bartend?"

They blink back at me, evidently taken with my riveting speech. The werecheetah in a tight blue dress raises her hand. "Me and Grace used to work at a bar."

"Close enough, come on up here, you're on."

"Seriously," the hyena asks. "This is your plan?"

"No, dickless," I say. I motion around. "You see all these humans?"

"Yeah?"

"They need protection and they need to stay here. Whatever is out there mutilated one of our kind. What do you think it'll do to them?" I scan the group, searching for anyone looks somewhat bright. Except for the girls who agreed to bartend, none of them scream Rhodes Scholars.

"You, you, you, and you. Take a team of three and hit the clubs along this strip. Most people around here are out for the night. Keep them safe."

They nod as one and disperse. "What about us?" Houndstooth asked.

"Yeah," Orange Polo says. "He's a Leader and we're just as strong as these guys."

The hyena hears him and cackles on his way out. Under other circumstances, I'd laugh right along with him. Except, I'm supposed to be all motivational and shit. "You guys patrol the area. Hit the streets, the beach, the alleys. Anything you find that doesn't look right, you *call*, get me? The world is counting on you."

I don't quite finish with a straight face. Except these guys, especially Houndstooth, are used to having their egos stroked. They take in my bull, allowing it to fill their lungs and puff their chests.

"Yes, sir," they reply.

And fucking salute.

Really? How has nothing eaten them yet?

I leap over the bar and march toward the door. Emme's voice glues me in place. "Bren? What about me?"

My throat warms, down to my stomach and further south. I spit the words out through my teeth. "Emme, you're with me."

I take off, faster than I intend, the need to keep some distance between me and Emme clouding my common sense. I practically plow through the bouncers at the door. They're human so they don't say shit. Figures the vamps at the door would take off without letting anyone know.

"Bren, wait," Emme calls after me.

I force myself to stop at the corner. Emme reaches me, out of breath. "I'm sorry. I'm having trouble keeping up."

Of course, she is. She's not Celia who can outrun my ass. "No, I'm sorry. I just...you know I'm not used to this leadership crap."

She reaches for me, her two delicate hands giving mine a squeeze, and Jesus God, it's all I can do not to have sex with her against the building.

My neck practically creaks with how slow I swivel my head. Strands of her long, blond hair spill away from the clip to skim her shoulders and face, that same face I touched and kissed not long ago. Why did I have to kiss her? Now, I just want to kiss her more.

"You're doing great," she says. She smiles apologetically. "I just don't move as fast as you. Maybe it will be better if we take an Uber?"

"Werewolves don't Uber," I practically snarl.

Any human would run away screaming. Emme just smiles. She knows I'd never hurt her.

"Then we'll walk," she says. She glances down at our hands and gives another squeeze. "I think I can keep up if you help." She loses her smile. "Just don't let me go, okay?"

I swallow hard. "I won't," I promise.

It takes some doing to slow down. Hell, it takes some doing to breathe normally with Emme this close. We reach the next block. I'm moving fast, just not so fast that she can't keep up.

"There's something we need to talk about," she says.

Shit. Here we go.

Why'd you kiss me, Bren?

Why are you such a slut, Bren?

Can I straddle you in the next side street, Bren?

Oh, Bren. Oh, *Bren*. *Oh, Bren*!

I'll admit, the last few thoughts may have been uncalled for.

"There was something with us in Ted's apartment," Emme says. "Something that wasn't human."

I stop so fast, Emme loses her footing. I steady her just before she topples over. "And you're just telling me this now?" I ask.

Her cheeks flush pink. "I was sort of distracted back at the bar."

Because my tongue was waving hello to your tonsils? I can respect that.

She clears her throat, but not her blush. I move us further down the street, trying to give her a minute. "Ted didn't seem to notice. But the other *weres* in his complex did. When I left Ted's apartment, a few sensed it and went after it."

A couple walking their dog on the opposite street looks over at us when their little pup yips and barks hello. I ignore her and press Emme for more. "Is the complex called the Garden Center?"

"Yes," she says.

"Figures," I say. "That's where we're headed. It's where the *weres*, the ones I'm guessing went after that thing, are with Ted."

"I thought you said he was ripped to pieces," she says slowly.

"Oh, he was," I assure her. "The *weres* were nice enough to shove him into some sandwich bags."

My tidbit of knowledge doesn't go over well with Emme. "Did I say sandwich bags? I meant freezer size—the ones with the zipper lock," I add, hoping it makes her feel better. "They store body parts nicely."

Emme tries to swallow but doesn't quite make it. "I'll bet," she says.

"Tell me more," I say. "What feel did you get from that presence? *Were*, witch, ghoul?"

She makes a face. "A touch of evil," she replies.

"A touch?" I repeat.

She nods as if that's the best way she can describe it. "There was something very wrong about it. About it existing."

I give it some thought, edging Emme under a row of canopies when it starts to drizzle. "You thinkin' demon?"

"Not quite," she says. She stares down the street as if fighting to re-member exactly what she perceived. "It was a mix of sorts. Dark magic for certain, and the dread that accompanies demons, but not quite one thing for sure."

"That doesn't make a whole lot of sense," I tell her.

"I know. It didn't for me either. It also didn't make sense how Ted ig-nored it."

She inches her way from under the canopy when the rain eases to a stop, the way she takes me in better than any man deserves.

"There was something else," she admits. "Something that followed me to the bar."

It's all I can do not to lose it. "Let me get this straight. A dark pres-ence tried to kill you at Ted's..."

"I never said it tried to kill me," Emme interjects.

"...and when it couldn't, it followed you to the Hole?"

Emme ignores my escalating growls. "No. This wasn't the same thing I sensed at Ted's. That thing was dangerous. What appeared to follow me seemed lost, confused, and maybe a little scared."

"Are you telling me you felt sorry for the scary thing that followed you?"

Emme rubs her thumb along my skin and I instantly forget I'm supposed to be mad at her for being so naive.

"I wouldn't go that far," she replies. "It seemed innocent. I thought it was a wandering spirit with how little energy it carried. I turned around several times when I sensed it approach, I just never saw it."

"It didn't try to grab you?" I ask.

"No," she says. "It wasn't threatening, at least, I don't think so. It was just sort of there."

"And you never saw anything?" She shakes her head and I curse some more. "Emme, this whole thing sounds screwed up. That thing was stalking you, you could've been hurt, or worse."

"I don't think so," Emme says. "The vampire serving as bouncer at the door noticed it, too. If it were trying to kill me or was as dangerous as you claim, he would have protected me."

"Why the hell would you think that?"

Emme regards me like I'm missing something. "Misha is his master and he was told to look out for me."

Her voice trails as I all but leap out of my skin. "What's wrong?" she asks.

"That vamp you're so sure would have saved you?"

"Yes?" she asks.

"He wasn't at the door when we left, and he should've been. My boss did Misha a favor by hiring him." I look at her, taking in her innocence, and growing oh-so pissed that someone else, in addition to Ted, could have harmed her.

"Something took or lured that vamp from his post," I add. "I'm guessing it was that same something that followed you to the Hole."

Emme lets go of my hand and fumbles for her phone. "That's strange, it's dead," she says. "I always keep it charged."

My pace slows to a crawl. "Did it work earlier?"

She glances from me to the phone and back. "Yes. I spoke to Shayna and texted with Taran and Celia after I left Ted's."

I hold out my hand. "May I?"

Emme places the phone in my opened palm. I take a sniff and spit into the next drain we pass. "It's cursed." Her eyes widen. "Whatever followed you may not have scared you, Emme, but it should have. It was strong enough to curse your phone."

"Why?" she asks.

I furrow my brows. "So, you couldn't call for help."

"I realize that, Bren," she says. "What I mean is, why me?"

"Why not? For all you're the quiet and shy one of the Weird Girls, you're still a Weird Girl. Anyone with an ounce of magic knows that."

"Wird," Emme clarifies, appearing insulted. "Our last name is Wird, and you know it."

"I'm not trying to offend you," I say. "But the Weird Girls are what you and your sisters are known as. You're one of the powerful four who flipped the supernatural world on its ass. Like it or not, you are a threat, and something the bad guys can use as leverage."

"They really see me as such?"

Emme's not really asking. She's just having trouble believing it. It makes sense. She's never given the credit she's earned or deserves.

"Yeah," I say, wishing it wasn't true. "Things will keep coming after you, Emme. Now, more than ever." I drag my hand through my hair. "I know you were counting on your meeker personality to keep you in the shadows, and I think for the most part it's worked. Shayna, with her sword skills and how she skips into danger, Celia with her agility and strength, Taran, well, just being Taran, they were harder to ignore. Everyone pegged you as the weakling and follower. And when you were with Liam, they viewed him as your much-needed protector. Now though, you have everyone's attention. Look at how many missions you've been a part of."

"I guess," she hesitantly agrees.

"And look at who calls you their fam," I add.

"Aric," she mumbles.

"Yeah, only the most powerful *were* in history, who's fathered a child with your sister that's destined to save the world." I rub my chin. "Em, for all you've bowed out and allowed your family the spotlight, you never stood a chance, kid."

"Please don't call me that," she says, suddenly looking up.

"What? A kid?" The hurt in her small features makes me want to slap myself upside the head. "You know I don't mean it like that."

Emme quiets and plays with her hair, something she does when she's feeling shy or scared. "So much of this doesn't make sense," she says. "I can understand being used as leverage against Celia and Aric if I'm caught. But what do I have to do with the witches who were found on the Nevada side? I'm certain I don't know them. I didn't go to witch school. That was all Taran and she's not even here."

"I don't know. All I know is that you're not leaving my side tonight. Come on, let's get where we're going and figure this shit out."

Chapter Seven

Bren

The apartment complex was pretty decent. If I'm right, Aric bought it a few years back to help the *weres* displaced during the war. Single *weres* take residence in the smaller apartments on the upper levels, while the larger residences with direct access to the courtyard are mostly made up of young families. It's a nice, modern building: clean, well-kept, except for Ted's place.

Holy shit, what a dump!

Fast food bags and old pizza boxes litter the floor. And what reeks of old cheese floats in a clogged kitchen sink. The best part of the place is the giant hole where Emme must have sent this loser flying. It allows air in, and more importantly, some of the nastier smells out.

The *weres* who gave chase linger in the small living room. There are two beat-up couches and a broken recliner with too many stains to count and too many stinks to name. No one is sitting. Smart *weres*. A human would need an STD test and a shot of penicillin if he or she wandered anywhere near that recliner. Hell, I'm surprised it hasn't killed a passing squirrel.

The cougar who met us at the entrance guides us inside. "We didn't clean up in case ya needed to look for evidence.

I kick a pizza box out of my way. "Yeah. Thanks for that."

I shoot Emme a glance. She finds someplace else to look. If Ted were still alive, I'd seriously wipe the floor with that fucker. Kill two birds with one stone, feel me?

The cougar motions to a small hall. "The body parts are in there," he says.

He leads us into a bathroom, barely big enough to allow the three of us in and with some elbow room. Mold and mildew spread across the subway tile. Toothpaste stains and used floss plaster the sink, wall, and floor. Nice to see dental hygiene was a priority.

I take a good look at the tub and immediately block Emme's view. "Christ," I mutter. "You sure you want to be in here?"

"No," she says. "But if I can help, I should be."

"You sure, miss?" The cougar makes a face. "Your boyfriend ain't looking too good."

"He wasn't her boyfriend," I tell him, before Emme can.

The snarl to my voice catches me off guard. I avoid looking at Emme and edge closer to the tub. A shit-ton of baggies and Ted bits are stacked to the rim. I cross my arms. "Where exactly did you find him?"

"The beach. Close to the dock where dem rich people keep their boats," the cougar tells me.

"He didn't *change*," I say.

Emme clears her throat. "Ted was, um, not dressed when I threw him out of the window."

I roll my eyes. "Don't remind me. What I mean is, he didn't *change* into his beast form."

Emme shuffles behind me. "That's odd. He should have if something was trying to kill him. It would have made him stronger."

"Unless he was still unconscious from you throwing his ass out," the cougar points out.

All the color drains from Emme's face. "Oh, my God. Bren, I killed Ted."

I peg the cougar with a narrowed gaze. He backs up and bumps into the toilet. "No, you didn't, Emme," I say.

"But if he was unconscious, he couldn't protect himself," she insists.

Emme is the worst liar ever. Like, even worse than Celia, and Celia is embarrassingly bad at it. And I'm not even talking about the "I'm guilty" sign with an arrow pointing down she's currently waving over her head. Have these girls learned nothing from hanging out with me?

"Emme, you didn't kill Ted," I bite out.

She places her hand on my arm, her eyes pleading. "How do you know?"

I don't. I just don't want to implicate you for murder. "Because it takes more than a fall three stories down to knock out a *were*." I cough into my shoulder. "Did he make a noise when he hit the ground?"

"Yeah," the cougar pushes. "When you cracked his skull against the concrete sidewalk all dem stories down, did he make any sound? Even a gurgle?"

I think the cougar is trying to help. He isn't.

Emme beams. "He cursed," she said quickly. "I remember him swearing quite a bit."

Thank Christ. I shrug. "See? It's fine."

"I was sure she knocked his punk ass out," a female calls out from the living room. "Don't worry, honey," she says. "He would've deserved that shit anyway."

"Oh, jeeze," Emme squeaks, covering her face.

I change the subject, needing to get this over with, and Emme out of here. "What'd you find at the scene?"

The cougar whips out his phone and shows us several shots. I take it back. He shows *me* several shots. Emme stops looking when she takes a gander at the first sets of chunks.

"There wasn't a lot of clean up," the cougar says. "Just the meat. The sand absorbed all the blood and body fluids"

Emme gags. I hold up a hand. "I can see that, man." I point to the sections of bone. "See that. All the bones are the same size. The same as human size. He didn't *change* at all."

"You saying he didn't put up a fight?" the cougar asks.

I flip through the photos. "I'm saying a lot things," I admit. "He either couldn't fight or didn't want to, which is bullshit. We're *weres*, fighting is what we do."

"Damn, right," the motley crew in the living room calls out. Several fist bumps and high-fives follow.

I focus on the pictures and keep going. "My guess is he couldn't fight. Magic or something else overpowered him."

My focus shifts to Emme as I talk to the cougar, raising my voice slightly so the other *weres* know I'm speaking to them, too. "You only felt one presence, right?"

The crew in the living room mutters in agreement. The cougar nods. "That's right," he says. "It smelled wrong, you feel me? Smelled off, like it didn't belong here. But there was only one we tracked."

"Demon?" I ask. "Or one of its spawn?"

"Yes and no," the cougar says. "It felt wrong, like a demon, but not exactly a demon. Not its spawn either," he adds quickly before I can ask. "It was hateful and angry and shit. Almost what you'd expect to find in a vengeful ghost who's stuck here with something to prove."

Emme nods. Yeah, it's pretty much what she told me. I go through the pictures again, pausing when I notice something in the sand. "What's this?" I ask.

Swirls, almost like a design, form patterns along the beach. "Don't know," the cougar says. "They look witch-like, symbols and such, but they ain't."

Emme edges closer. I expand the photos to avoid her seeing more of the carnage. "They do look like magical patterns. Pretty," she says. "But it's not something that could conjure or harm."

"You sure?"

Emme nods. "When Taran was in witch school, I often helped her study. Runes, symbols, and objects of power needed to be positioned in a certain order. This is more artwork than spell craft."

"Still might be worth checking out," I reply. I hand the cougar back his phone. "Moving on. Did you see anything else or leave anything behind?"

"Nope. Nothing for any humans to find." He motions to the tub. "We knew we had to get the body back, we just didn't want any of him back at our place. Sorry we messed up your murder scene or whatever the hell."

"You didn't mess up the scene because Ted wasn't killed here. And based on how much evil this thing spewed, you'd have sensed it prior to today had it shown."

Another set of "damn rights," from the *weres* and a nod from the cougar tell me I'm right.

I inch closer when Emme tenses. There's nowhere clean to stand and not much room. Had Ted owned a vacuum and some cleanser, and maybe if he wasn't such a lazy bastard, this would have been a pretty swinging place and what I had to do wouldn't be as bad.

But he was lazy and what's left of him is in this disgusting bathroom.

There's not much blood on the floor, the sandwich bags did a decent job keeping everything in, but the nasty meter is hitting an all-time high. The smell pre-Ted mutilation was bad. I picked up on it the moment we reached the second level. With the mutilation...let's just say I'm pretty shocked Emme's still vertical.

I fall on one knee, careful to avoid the splatter of blood that escaped. Using care, I sort through the packages, trying to see if there's anything I can use. "Is there any way this is more than just Ted?" I ask. Hell, if there's more than just one body part mixed in here, we have ourselves a whole other set of problems.

"It's him," both Emme and the cougar answer.

"How do you—" I push aside some smaller packages when a larger one catches my interest. "One, two—Holy *shit*. This bastard had three testicles?"

"Yes," Emme and the cougar reply.

The fact that Emme answers, makes me want to shove what's left of Ted in the microwave and set it to high. But I won't because I'm classy and definitely, I repeat, definitely not jealous.

I lift one of the three bags. "I've heard about this," I say.

"Yeah," the cougar agrees. "But it's not something I want to be known for."

"I don't mean I've heard about it because of Ted," I say. I shake the bag, remembering Danny yammer on about the details once. "This condition or whatever the hell."

"He had a condition?" Emme asks. "Was it caused by extra testosterone?"

"Nice guess, but not exactly," I say. I toss the baggy aside and reach for a larger piece of Ted. It's a wrist, the edge is crushed and badly bruised. "Not counting Aric, who *changed* at like two months of age, the strongest *weres* usually *change* into their beast forms by the age of six months. The weaker ones, closer to a year."

The cougar shrugs. "We know that. Where are you goin' with this, alpha?"

I don't like being addressed by a title, but there are worse things the cougar can call me. He is only trying to show respect, so I let it slide.

"There's this condition weak *weres* get. It's rare, as in, once in two lifetimes rare. No one likes to talk about it because those *weres* usually die while the female is still pregnant. It's known as nose blindness. Those *weres*, those who make it I mean, *change* three-hundred and sixty-six days from birth, just about missing being *were* completely. Ted was one of these."

"You know this how, alpha?" the cougar asks. "Because of his three stones?"

I nod and lift another damaged piece of limb, an ankle, also bruised and the bones broken or close to it. "Instead of developing more testosterone, the fetus doesn't release enough. The dormant inner beast of the fetus tries to compensate and grows another teste, to maintain the beast form attempting to develop and try to strengthen the fetus. But the weakness is still there, get me? It worsens the longer the pregnancy lasts and results in nose blindness."

"Oh, I understand," Emme says. She looks to the cougar who doesn't quite figure it out. "Ted couldn't smell."

"Ted couldn't sense jack," I agree. "It's called nose blindness because the sense of smell never develops. But it affects all the other senses, too, reducing them to subpar human levels or less."

The *weres* in the other room gasp. As a species known for our badassness, they've never imagined something so horrible. I get it. Our senses are among the main things that make us who we are. They help us hunt, protect, and makes us the formidable beings we are. It's probably why

Ted was such a dick. He felt the need to make everyone feel less than him since he was less than what he was supposed to be. But it was this pseudo dominance that likely caused his death.

I rise with the largest piece of evidence in the cluster. Emme backs away and toward the living space where the other *weres* who gave chase continue to wait. She stops when I don't follow.

"It's why I sensed what I did, and so did the others," she tells me. "I could because of my magic. Ted didn't have it in him to sense anything."

"Yup. And another reason why this dump didn't bother him as much as it should," I agree.

"But why did it kill him?" Emme asks.

I bend and exchange the bag for another. The evidence is smaller, but the bruising is more pronounced.

"Bren?" she says.

I don't want to tell her. I'm already pissed. Saying it makes it worse. "My guess?" I ask. She nods. "It thought you were together and wanted to get anyone who might protect you out of the way."

Her features reflect her shock and her fear. "Don't worry," I say. "Aric is with Ceel. Shayna and Koda are together, and Taran is causing yet another international incident on the other side of the globe."

Emme meets me square in the face. "That's not who I'm worried about right now," she whispers.

Her reply hits me in the chest like a punch. *Nothing's going to happen to me, sweet one...And I'll be damned if I let anything hurt you.*

Emme glides out of the bathroom and into the hall where the cougar is waiting. The cougar shadows her. I catch him eyeing up Emme and just about slap him upside the head with a piece of Ted.

I don't like how close the cougar is to Emme and step between them when we enter the living room. "Here," I say. I brush what has to be a good inch of Cheeto dust off a stool and motion to it.

Emme grimaces when her focus skips to the plastic baggie in my hand.

Oh, yeah. *That.* "It's okay if you want to sit someplace else," I say.

"No," she replies softly. "I want to be with you."

I puff out my chest and all but beat it with my fists. "Well, someone around here's gotta protect you."

Although I'm trying to pretend what she said and how she said it, didn't affect me, it actually did. Damn.

I turn to address the crowd, thinking I masked my reaction well enough until the bear in the corner holds up his fist. "Yeah, dog," he tells me.

Thanks, dipshit. "All right, folks," I say. "Listen up. What we have here is—"

A weasel near the infected recliner whips his hand up, interrupting me. "Ted?" he offers.

"It wasn't a question," I say. Christ, Koda gets the witches and *this* is what I have to work with?

I start again. "We have an unknown enemy among us. You see this?" I reach into the bag and yank out what's left of a knee and accidently splash Emme with leftover Ted bits. "Oops. Sorry there, Em."

A female rips off a somewhat clean paper towel and passes it to Emme. Emme graciously accepts, but not without a slight lurch of her stomach.

It's about then, I start to lose the room.

"Like I was saying, we have an unknown enemy among us," I say. I add some power behind my voice. It's what Aric does when he addresses the pack, and look at that, it works. I hand off the bag to the cougar, holding the knee and pointing to different parts. "What do you see?" I roll my eyes when the weasel lifts his hand again. "Besides blood, muscle, tissue, and bone?"

No one answers. Oh, boy. I swipe the skin and try again. "Bruises," the cougar says. "Lots of them."

"Yup," I agree. "Whatever killed Ted crushed multiple parts of him, almost evenly and at the same time."

"What the hell kind of thing can do that?" someone asks.

"And then rip him apart into such small pieces so quickly?" a female adds. She glances around the room. "We were right on top of that thing. It didn't have time to work Ted up like you say it did. It must have been magic, a curse or something else."

"No, you would have smelled—." I stop mid-sentence when I catch the scent of something I shouldn't catch. I sniff again, just to make sure.

"What is it, alpha?" the cougar asks.

"Do me a favor," I say to him. "Pour me a glass of water."

He does and passes me the glass. I take whiff. All the funk from Ted's place interferes with the aroma of the water. I have to practically shove my nose into the glass to catch a better trace.

The *weres* lean in, waiting for me to break down the complexities of my theory in the most eloquent way I can. And I do. "This shit's fucked up."

I place the glass down and roll the decapitated knee in my hand, specifically where the bruising is most pronounced. Emme tilts forward, whispering low. "Can you elaborate, please?"

"This is tap water," I say, motioning to the glass.

The *weres* exchange glances. I'm starting to think they're doubting my brilliance. "We know that, boss," the weasel says slowly.

Great. Now I'm the one looking like a moron. "If Ted bathed..." I take another gander at the room. "And that's a mighty big 'if,' he would have used tap water."

"That's right," the cougar says.

"And had he gone swimming in the lake or had that creature dragged Ted into the lake, he would smell like freshwater."

"He wasn't wet," the female in the front says. "Only moist from sweat and body fluid."

"What do you smell, Bren?" Emme asks. She clutches her small purse against her, as if it can somehow protect her from the gore. "*Is it* water?"

"Yeah, it is," I say. "Saltwater."

The weasel cocks an eyebrow. "We're a pretty long ways off from any ocean, boss."

"I know. But it's what I smell." I toss him the knee.

He takes it and takes a sniff, then another one, and another one after that. There's a reason I'm known for my nose. I pick up on more than the average *were*. "He's right," the weasel says. "Dang. I wouldn't have caught it if he hadn't pointed it out."

The *weres* pass the body part around, all taking their time with it, their gazes lighting up when they catch traces of the ocean.

Emme slips off the stool. "Does this help you identify what it might be?"

"No," I admit. "It just makes this thing that much messier."

"How so?" she asks.

"Whatever is out there is a carnivore," I reply. "All those pieces weren't just a show of strength. It broke up Ted to eat him."

"To...eat...him?" Emme asks.

The *weres* nod, they get it. Hey, and look at Emme go. She doesn't puke, no matter how much she looks like she wants to. I pat her back, that's my girl.

"Y'all. Something's out there," I say to the group. "Those with families, stay here and watch your own. Everyone else, split up into groups and start patrolling. Whatever is out there won't stop with Ted. It's hungry and still needs to eat."

Chapter Eight

Bren

Emme and me hit the beach and head to where Ted was found. On the way, I call Koda and spill the details we uncovered.

"Any chance there's a species of wereoctopus we're not aware of?" I ask.

"Don't be a dumbass," Koda growls at me. "The only species of marine life are weredolphins 'cause their mammals and weresharks cause they're predators."

"So, how do you explain the bruises and crushed bones, sugar tits?" I ask. "The only thing I know that could do anything close to what happened to Ted are weregorillas or something in the ape family. Ted's condition tells me there'd have to be an entire troop, except Emme and the others insist there was only one creature."

"Damned if I know," Koda responds. "And damned if I know how these witches are involved."

Emme wraps her arms around herself and curls inward. She's freezing. I tuck my phone beneath my chin and pass her my flannel shirt.

One of the females who lives in the complex has a daughter close to Emme's size. She lent Emme jeans to trade out for her skirt. The jeans fit her frame well enough, and initially Emme was warm. Now that we're on the sand, and the wind is picking up, she's probably regretting not borrowing a jacket.

"Thank you," she says.

My shirt is huge on her. I watch her roll up the sleeves and lift her hair, so it falls against her shoulders. She gave up on keeping her hair up. That's okay. Emme has the best hair around.

The wind lifts the strands like gold streaming waves that flow around her. She looks dab smack in the middle of a photo shoot. But Emme isn't the model type. Her features aren't chiseled nor can she strike a pose. That doesn't mean she isn't beautiful.

"Did you hear me, numb nuts?" Koda asks.

"No, bitch," I fire back. "The reception is bad. Repeat, asshole. I said, repeat."

Koda sighs. Even from here, he knows I'm lying. He passes the phone to Shayna, muttering something about what a waste of life I am.

"Hey, dudes," Shayna chimes in.

"Tell him I'm a *sexy* waste of life," I instruct.

Shayna doesn't laugh, like I expect, and her typical glee is absent in her voice. I hit the speaker button so Emme can listen in. "It's getting worse, isn't it?"

"Yeah, it is," Shayna says. "The witch parts we found all belonged to Lesser witches. Some have been dead only a few days. Others, well, it's safe to say this stuff has been going on a long time, peeps."

Emme huddles into the flannel shirt. "You said they were Lessers?"

"Uh, huh," Shayna answers. "Not full witches nor were they still in school."

"Were they ever in school?" I ask.

"Yes. One even attended Genevieve's school, but she never graduated," Shayna explains. "The other witches studied elsewhere, but also never achieved the title of full witch. Genevieve made inquiries with other covens by sharing their faces." She groans. "Or what's left of their faces. Like I mentioned, some of these bodies have been out here a long time. Four were identified by the head witch in the Tri-state area and two by a head witch out of Boston."

"And none of them graduated?" Emme asks.

"Nope," Shayna answers. "In fact, most didn't make it past their first few years of study. From what Genevieve says, none of the ladies possessed much magic or skill."

"So, they officially couldn't belong to any coven," Emme reasons.

"That's right, and therefore didn't have the benefits that come with belonging to a coven," Shayna says. "Sure, they had head witches responsible for keeping them in line, but they weren't considered 'sisters' or welcomed to their functions."

I kick a rock out of my way as we continue forward, sending it flying into the water. "Without a coven, these Lessers were easy targets," I mumble.

"Yes, and no," Shayna says. "Witches are like vamps, and *weres*. Even if they don't belong to a coven, clan, or pack, the big bosses are still responsible for their actions and their safety. The head witches in Boston and New York are angry with Genevieve for letting anything happen to them. Coven or not, they still had a connection to the deceased, and while they're still technically residents on the east coast, witches are supposed to watch out for their own, no matter where they go."

Emme rubs her hands. "Shayna, I can understand their anger, these women were brutally murdered. But they're casting the blame on the wrong person."

"Pfft. Tell me about it, Emme," Shayna says. "One of the witches materialized while we were here and all but cursed Genevieve out. She's demanding Genevieve make financial and magical arears. Koda told Genevieve she wasn't obliged to. The witch told Koda to butt out. Koda became testy—you know Puppy doesn't like being yelled at—and told her to eff off and to remove the broomstick she has rammed up her ass— I made him apologize, but you can tell he really hated doing it. Anyway, Koda made it clear that this was *were* territory and that we would handle it."

"I did," Koda agrees with a growl. "So, handle it, Bren. We've got this side. You have that side. Get this shit worked out."

"Good luck, dudes," Shayna says, and disconnects.

Emme shoves the shoes she wore deeper into her small purse. "The other head witches in the country are trying to get rid of Genevieve."

"Yeah, and this is a good excuse to do it," I say. I reach for Emme's hand without thinking. Everything we learn is that much worse. I wish she wasn't a part of it.

After one hell of a look at my hand, she meets my face, offering the start of another heart-battering smile. I lead her forward before I allow that smile to be my undoing. I have a job to do, and part of my responsibility is making sure nothing happens to this sweet thing beside me.

Some of the *weres* back at the complex wanted to come with us. I wouldn't allow it. It's not that I just want Emme to myself, it's because of what's out here.

Those *weres* already have a feel for what this thing is. They're our best chance to keep the humans around here safe. The other side of the coin is, I don't know them. There wasn't time to interrogate each one to see if they played a part in what happened. It would be stupid on their end, sure. They know who Emme is to Aric, and maybe what she can do on her own. But Ted seemed to know too, and it didn't stop him from pulling some major bullshit moves on Emme.

"Genevieve is getting too strong, isn't she?" Emme asks. "It's why the other witches are coming down so hard on her."

My gaze trails to the left. I take in how the full moon reflects along the passing waves, and how it feels to have Emme so close. Blood, death, and decapitated kneecaps aside, this is what some shmuck might refer to as a romantic stroll. I just wish I wasn't the shmuck making the reference. For what has to be the hundredth time tonight, I remind myself that this is Emme. *Emme.* Not someone I can just share a few hours with alone in bed.

"They're all strong," I say, taking way too long to answer. "Genevieve is among the most powerful of her kind. So is Aric, and fucking Misha. And they all reside here in Tahoe, a beacon of power and magic. Those greedy bastards, the head witches and master vamps throughout the country, want this territory for themselves. They're willing to take out any of the bosses, or at the very least discredit them if it means one step closer to claiming Tahoe."

I stop when we reach the spot where Ted took his last dying breath. "This is it, isn't it?" Emme asks.

"Yup," I respond.

Emme releases my hand a little too soon and much to my dislike. I don't sense anything in the surrounding area yet. That doesn't mean I want her venturing far.

She circles the area where Ted's body was found. The way he was ripped to pieces and how those pieces were thrown apart, it's a fairly large section of space to cover. Except there she is, her steps careful, avoiding the spots where the pieces landed as if as visible as the moon above. For someone who doesn't have my nose, she has astonishing instincts when it comes to magic.

I walk to the opposite side, noting the section where the marks remain. There are swivels and swerves and... "Hm," I say.

Emme makes her way to me, careful not to disrupt the patterns. "What do you see?"

"Handprints. Two of them." I point to two spots in the section of swivels.

"I don't really see them," Emme admits.

"Between the breeze sweeping all the sand around and all the *weres* that were here to pick up the parts, they're hard to make out, but that's what they are." I crouch and take in a long breath of air. There's that salty scent again. It's lighter here than what was on the knee cap. Still, I catch enough before it disappears in the breeze.

Something about the handprints catch my attention. "They're not big, and not *were*," I say. I tilt my head in Emme's direction. "They're too small. Our females tend to have long hands and fingers. These are too short and stubby for *weres*." I make a face. "They're also smooth, as in no prints. Shit. They're even different hands, both lefties."

"Then there are probably more individuals involved than we realize," Emme says.

"Yeah," I say. "That would make the most sense. Just something about it doesn't feel right."

"This whole thing doesn't feel right," she adds.

"That's for damn sure," I mutter.

Emme takes a few steps forward, studying the patterns hard. "How can you tell those are handprints for certain?" she asks. "Prints are hard to see even under the best circumstances."

I shrug. "Subtle pressure against the sand can lead to even small creases. This thing, or things, left a hell of a lot of pressure, but no creases."

Emme smiles, pride finding its way into her voice. "You notice every-thing," she says. "I guess that's why you're the best tracker in the pack."

And holy fuck, now I'm the one blushing.

I push off the sand and brush off my jeans. "Come on. I can't make heads or tails of these markings. Let's head further down and see if we can pick up on something else."

"Are you...blushing?" Emme asks.

"Fuck no. Wolves don't fucking blush," I say. "Just windy is all. Fucking bastard wind. Always shows up when you don't fucking need it. Fuck."

I stomp ahead before I realize I'm leaving Emme behind. "You all right?' I ask, stopping dead in my tracks.

"Yes, just thinking," she says.

She seems lost in her thoughts, not exactly rushing to catch up. By the time she reaches me, she's downright frowning. "The masters will even-tually go after the other masters; it's part of their bloodthirsty character traits and what's kept the vampires wealthy and in power for centuries."

"They are greedy bastards," I agree.

"And the head witches are also gunning for each other," she adds.

"That's right," I tell her.

"What about the *weres*? The other alphas? Will they go after Aric?"

"Em, every *were* with a clue should fear Aric." I blow out a breath. "And after all that crap that happened with Celia, most are downright terrified." My voice lowers when I tell her what I do. "That doesn't mean another kind of supernatural won't try to mess with him and what he has."

As well as try for you and your sisters.

Emme stares hard at the sand, careful to avoid a section of broken shells and rock. She knows where my thoughts are headed. "It would be unwise for the master vampires and head witches to take on Misha and

Genevieve, as well as Aric. It's not just their prowess or skill, they have allies and connections worldwide."

"Yeah, and those connections keep growing." My boot crushes a brittle stone, my weight too much for it despite its length and width. "There are rumors going around Genevieve is going to claim the entire west coast as her own. She has Nevada and California, and she's targeting Oregon and Washington next."

"There's already a head witch in that territory," Emme says carefully.

"I know. Lumina. But she's all power and no flair from what I hear." I rub my nose when I catch a trace of something else. "Aric's hoping Lumina will step down. He doesn't like her and considers Vieve a good leader and ally. For as much as Aric and Vieve do not always see eye to eye, they have a decent working relationship and he respects her."

"Do you think he respects Genevieve enough to support her acquisition of the remaining states?"

"No. He won't go that far. If he did, it would cause a riff with the *weres* in Oregon and Washington," I reply. "Aric flat out told Genevieve he won't back her if it comes down to a duel."

"A duel? That would be terrible," Emme says. "Two witches fighting, especially two head witches, is never a good thing."

"It'll be one hell of a fight," I agree with a nod.

"You sound certain there'll be one," Emme says.

"That's because I am. Lumina scheduled one for October 30th. Vieve has given her until the twenty-nineth to back down and surrender before she curses her ass."

"Lumina is strong, you say," Emme replies. "Are you sure Genevieve is stronger?"

At my nod she asks, "So why would Lumina challenge her to a duel? She's not only risking her territory, she's risking her life."

I shrug. "If I were Vieve's rival, hell, or Misha's, I'd take them out before they grew more powerful than they are. They ain't gettin' any weaker."

"From a warmonger perspective, it does make sense," Emme begins.

"But?" I ask. I stop when another scent catches my interest.

"But nothing. I suppose I'm just confused. With so many adversaries and supernatural muscle flexing occurring on a regular basis, why would anyone bother with me?"

My attention focuses on the row of rocks lining the edge along the road. "It's like I said, Emme, the alphas may not be dumb enough to mess with Aric directly, but you're an indirect way to him."

Damn. For all I didn't want to remind her of this, there I go, flapping my gums.

"What are you looking at?" she asks.

"Something that shouldn't be here," I reply.

Another trickle of that scent cuts through the air with the next rush of wind. Emme starts for the direction I'm eyeing. I don't let her.

"Stay put," I warn.

I jog up to the set of rocks. Most of these boulders have been here forever, with one exception. A large flat stone lays against several tons of larger, rounder boulders. Sure, it's the same color as the rest, and most would walk past it, thinking it belongs. 'Cept that it doesn't.

The position is odd. So is the shape compared to the rest. It was dragged from somewhere else and specifically placed here. I'm sure of it.

"Humph," I say. "It's a damn door."

Emme tilts her head. She's seeing what I'm seeing.

That smell I caught moments before trickles out between the cracks. I pace back and forth. Yeah, there it is, along with a rather pathetic scent of magic.

I step back. The lines I'd expect dragged along the sand aren't there. It may be a door, but it's not acting like one. There's no reasonable way to get inside. I take a chance and climb to the top. The tip of the flat stone isn't that large. I settle into a sitting position and place my heels on it, pushing hard.

This bastard is a lot heavier than it looks. It doesn't so much as creak.

I grip the edges and give it a shove. Shit. Unlike the stones along the sand I crushed with my weight, this thing is no joke.

Well, neither am I.

Stubborn has its advantages and I'm not giving up until this thing tips over and hits the ground.

My molars grind as I try another shove, and another, adjusting my hips to position better beneath it.

Sweat pours down my chest and back. Inside me, my wolf barks and yips, pumping me up and giving me all that we have to move this thing.

A dull ache builds from my feet and crawls up my joints, adding enough pressure to break my bones. This boulder isn't budging. I'm ready to try something else when I feel it give and it shifts.

That's right. Who's your daddy, bitch?

With all my strength, all my power, I push through the agony puncturing my legs and give one last hard push.

The weight falls away from my feet. I swerve around and kick up into a standing position, my hands lifted in unmatched glory. I am *were*. I am omnipotent. I am victorious.

Below me, Emme walks forward...and stands beside the rock she evidently lifted and placed aside with her *force*.

My hands lower. I am a moron, that's what I am.

"Are you okay, Bren?" she calls. She points to the rock. "It looked really heavy, so I thought I'd help."

"Er, thanks," I mutter.

Even from here with this low lightning I catch her blush. "Sorry," she squeaks. "I didn't mean to emasculate you or anything."

I hop down and land in the sand beside her. "The important thing is you're not rubbing it in." I flick the flashlight app on my phone and pass it to Emme. "Come on. Whatever you do, *do not* leave my side."

Chapter Nine

Bren

The opening to the cave is big enough for us to walk through side by side. It's a tight squeeze, but we manage well enough. A few yards in, now it's just tight, dark and dank, with that smell. Salty, yeah, bitter, too, and something else that I find familiar.

It's like we're going in circles, one bend leading down to another, the sand growing more wet with each push ahead. I'm not sure how far we are from the surface. My guess, about twenty feet.

I'm holding strong to Emme's hand, not wanting to lose her. It's what superheroes and kick-ass, manly-males do.

It's what I tell myself, and what my wolf nudges me to do. Except I think he's morphing us into some kind of pussy. Nah, we're too alpha for that crap. He's just watching out for her. For sure it's the latter. Besides, even if it wasn't, I can't do anything about it now. Or that kiss.

I steal a quick look at Emme. But at some point, I'll have to.

"Do you think something is hiding in here?" Emme whispers. "Or perhaps there's clues that will help us determine what's happening?"

"For sure," I say. "Whatever is in here, or was in here, has remnants of that salty smell I picked up earlier. There's also a lot of something else, magic. Some strong, some pathetically weak and almost laughable."

"Are you suggesting Lesser magic?" Emme asks.

A light bulb goes off. "Yeah," I say. "Like seriously weak loser Lesser magic."

Emme sweeps her hair behind her ears. Man, she has to stop doing all that sexy-cute stuff in front of me.

"Don't be mean, Bren," she says quietly. "The Lesser witches can't help the magic they're born with, and some, no matter how hard they try, will never hone their skills. They walk away from witch school in shame, never achieving their goals and never securing a coven."

Emme has a thing about her, she never wants anyone's feelings hurt, even if that someone isn't around to hear it. It's endearing and attractive, maybe a little too much for a wolf like me.

Her eyes light up when I reach for her face. I reach closer, carefully, but instead of stroking her gently, like my beast and I think we're ready to, I flick a large centipede from her hair.

She jumps when she sees just how many legs the little bastard has. I snatch her close to keep her from hitting the cave and mash a few more insects that...damn. There're some serious amount of legs in here.

"Oh, gosh. Oh, no. Oh, gosh. Oh, no."

Emme is jumping up and down and flicking bugs off her arms and shoulders. I catch one she flicks in the air by the tail and take a sniff. I take another, ignoring the pinchers the pissed-off little bugger snaps by my nose.

Emme freezes. "Are you hungry or something?"

"No." I point to the bug. "What? You think I'm trying to eat him?"

"It's really close to your face," she points out.

"I have standards, Em." I toss the bug when it pinches my bottom lip, pausing when I catch a really good whiff close to my nose. I pass my tongue over my lip, the taste mixed with the smell giving me a glimpse of what might be happening and further validating Emme's suspicions that I'm a bug-eating freak.

She fumbles through her purse and drops a shoe that's sticking out. "I think I have some peanut butter crackers in here."

I take the stupid crackers, but only 'cause I don't want to offend her or anything. I pop one in my mouth and look around.

Emme shines a light up at the ceiling. She doesn't take what she finds very well and muffles a scream.

The ceiling is alive with bugs, creepy crawly bugs, shoving each other aside as they search the sand for food. That's right, *sand.*

Emme looks from the ceiling to me a few times before she settles on my face. "We're *under* the lake?"

"Yup," I say. "When we went in, we must have crossed through some kind of magical air bubble."

"Should you howl for the *weres*?" she asks.

I shake my head. "No. We can't risk popping the bubble, and my *call* will definitely do it."

She eases closer to me. "Bren, a Lesser witch can't cast a spell like this."

"No," I agree. "But a large group might be able to." I look at her, not wanting to admit what happened. "Especially if they sacrificed enough blood and bodies."

"You mean enough of their own blood and bodies," she clarifies. "To conjure magic when you're not strong commands a self-sacrifice. But it's not like fasting or giving up something for Lent like Catholics do. It's vicious, cutting off all your fingers, sometimes a hand or even an arm. In the most extreme cases witches are known to sacrifice an eye."

I smile. Emme is almost as book smart as Dan. "You cracked more than a few of Taran's witch books, didn't you?"

"Taran really struggled in school." She shrugs, growing timid. "I wanted to help her, and maybe learn a little more about witches."

She jumps away when another creepy-crawly lands on top of her. "This doesn't appear to be a stable spell, no matter all the sacrifices used to cast it."

I pop another cracker in my mouth. Hey, they're pretty good. "There are a lot of holes in the spell," I agree. "But this place wasn't meant to last forever." I huff. "From what I can tell, it won't last the night."

A few more "plops" signal more bugs hitting the moist sand. "Bren, what are we going to do if this bubble breaks open?" Emme asks.

I polish off the last cracker and shove the plastic packaging into my pocket. "Swim," I suggest.

Panic sends her back toward the exit. "I don't know how to swim," she says. "You know as much."

I speak between bites. "Seeing all the crazy we go through on a monthly basis, you couldn't have squeezed in a few lessons?"

More bugs land on the sand when she shakes out her hair. "When would I have squeezed those lessons in, Bren? Between my shifts in Hospice or when I wasn't being chased by something rabid?"

"All right," I say. "I can see your point."

Emme lurches away from a spindly spider thing. More of that smell brushes against my nose, this time from the section of rock closest to Emme. I take a chance and give it a push. It gives a little. I press more of my weight into it, shoving my hands aggressively forward.

I step back, frowning when I see the indentations my hands made. It's like cement in here, the way it gets when it's close to hardening.

"The walls aren't real," Emme says. Her fingertips run along my handprints. She pushes at the center of the palm. It doesn't give, but that's not what she's trying to do. "Or they were, but like the rest of this place, they're coming undone."

I scratch at my beard and look around. "Em, what's the Latin word for open?"

"*Abre*, I think," she replies.

My hands grip the wall. "Okay, hold your breath."

"Hold my breath?" Her weight shifts from side to side as she maybe or maybe not questions my sanity. "Are you serious?"

"Yeah," I say. "What's the problem? You said it yourself, this place isn't real."

"What's my problem?" she demands. "Just because it's not real doesn't mean I'm ready for the remains to crumble around me and drown."

I push off the wall. "I sense you have some doubts here."

"You think?" The flashlight from my phone slams into my eyes when Emme rams her hands on her hips. For the first time ever, I can catch a small likeness to Taran. It's fair to say, I could've gone without catching that likeness.

"I know it seems like we went far, but I don't think we're more than a few feet from the surface."

She blinks back at me. "How many feet?"

I give a one shoulder shrug and look up. "I don't know, twenty, maybe forty?"

"Oh," she says.

Emme nods the way my last date did before she tried to run me over with her car. So what if I accidently hit on her MILF of a mom? These things happen.

"Only forty feet," she says. "Forgive me for sounding so irrational. I don't understand why I fretted so."

I laugh. Then again that broad wouldn't have used a word like "fretted."

"*Bren*," Emme says. "Don't laugh. I don't want to die."

My features soften and my laughter dwindles. "I won't let you, baby."

Emme stops moving. Slowly, very slowly, she adjusts her purse so it crosses her chest. She pinches her nose and gives a nod.

With that, I press my shoulder into the wall. "*Abre*," I mutter.

I shove harder, adding more command to my voice. "*Abre!*"

My beast perks up, the magic that houses and nurtures him, flowing through me. "*Abre!*"

Light floods the space as the walls expand. Insects rain down in sheets. I ignore the clicking sounds of pinchers at my ear, the scurry of their tiny limbs, and the bodies sliding down my back, clawing to hang on.

The wall isn't that hard to push, not like that flat stone it took Emme's *force* to set aside. It's more like how a human would shove a heavy piece of furniture across the floor.

Each motion, each budge forward, releases more of that smell, like opening a window and allowing the air to drift through in pungent bursts.

In a blur of soft motion, the layers of spells dissolve into one, stacking on top of each other to form a semi-circular wall of stone, the size of a small track field swarming with bugs. The insects topple all over themselves, scurrying through the wet sand at my feet where it's safe and where mounds of fresh food await them.

It's kind of cool. These bugs, lake critters, whatever you want to call them are different from what I've seen around Tahoe. You get used to the spiders and everything that burrows through the forest floor. For years, the paws of my beast have uncovered them as they kick through mounds of soil, rock, and dirt.

These little guys don't get to see the outside world. They get only specks of light from the moon and sun. I envy them, in a way. They don't have to belong. They're never judged. They just eat and live, like I think the rest of us are supposed to. Sure, there're bigger and badder things waiting to suck them down. For the most part, though, they just go along with their lives.

Yeah, they are cool. Maybe the rest of us can learn a thing or two from them.

Emme doesn't warm up to them like I do. To her credit, she's not screaming. Don't get me wrong, she looks like she's doing a really bad version of an African tribal dance, one that would get her kicked out of the tribe and possibly stoned, but a heck of an effort regardless.

She kicks at the air, flaps her arms, and shakes out her hair. I march over to her, brushing off some of the larger, livelier bugs intent on nesting behind her ears and making babies.

"You all right?" I ask.

"No," she squeaks. "My skin is crawling."

I help her out of my flannel and give it a shake. "No worries, it's just the bugs. Hey, look. These two are stuck together at the ass."

She glares at me. This time, it's not so cute. "I think it's intentional, Bren."

I give them another good look. "Oh, yeah." I elbow her playfully. "Must be mating season down here at the lake."

She covers her mouth like she's ready to puke. "Must be," she moans.

The moisture in the air clings the top Emme's wearing closer to her skin. She has on one of those padded bras that women with smaller curves wear.

It kind of surprises me. Emme doesn't need that. She's cute and nice and yeah, sexy, all on her own. I offer her back my flannel shirt, hoping in a way that she doesn't take it.

Emme is breathing really fast, her small chest lifting and falling as she trembles and continues to freak out. Her hands open and close as she threads them through the sleeves. She glances at them and rubs them together, carefully at first, then harder.

She looks up at me with her palms open. "They're sticky. Why are they sticky?"

I don't bother telling her it might be bug juice from all the crawlies she smacked at, she can probably guess as much. She does though, make a valid point.

Everything is sticky here, especially the air. Odd, since cool moisture is all we were exposed to on the way down. And it's not like Tahoe is known as a humid region. Hell, the only way to find humidity around here is by sticking your ass in a sauna.

My heels dig into the sand as I back away from the wall and the last few bugs find a new home. With the exception of the few moonbeams poking through the sandy ceiling, the opened area is plenty dark.

The surrounding walls resemble drifts of loose volcanic rock, nothing like the tough surfaces we avoided as we trekked through the cave. There's a light coat of dust, enough to muffle that scent I keep latching onto, yet not enough to erase it completely.

I take another deep breath, picking through all the aromas travelling through my nose, from the trickles of lake water, to the thin exoskeletons of the bugs, to Emme's perfume, and back to that smell. There's a bitterness to it, almost as pungent as the salty air I continue to sense, plus a tinge of something else.

My eyes fly open as I pinpoint exactly what this is.

Sex.

Lots and lots of sex.

I whip towards Emme. She continues to shake out her hair and bat at the invisible bugs she thinks are no-doubt burrowing through her scalp.

"Damn," I say.

She crinkles her nose and pokes her tongue out briefly. "I can taste the stickiness," she says. "It's everywhere. Can you taste it, too?"

"Uh, huh," I say, wishing we couldn't.

Emme pauses. "You know what it is, don't you?" she asks. I nod. She searches her surroundings. "Does this mean you know what this place is, too?"

"I have a pretty good idea," I say, and that's about it.

She gives another little tremble. "Aren't you going to tell me?"

"Ah, sure."

She stands there, waiting.

I stand there with my mouth firmly shut.

Emme is an angel. Innocent. Genuinely one of those types that believes in the good in others. She avoids the bad, all the time, just because she wants to see so much of that good.

I'm not one of those glass is half-full types. The glass is usually empty and bloody from the bastard that made me crack said glass over his skull.

It's safe to say I'm definitely not Emme. Nope. That doesn't mean I'm ready to come clean with the facts.

"Bren?" she says. "We're here to find answers." She shudders when another something lands on her head. It falls to the sand and scuttles away. "Just tell me what it is. Please. I'm not sure how much longer I can stay in this place."

"You don't want to know," I assure her.

"I do if it means finding out what's going on," she insists.

"Just tell me," she adds when I just look at her.

I give one last sniff. Yup. That's what it is. "It's a cat house, Emme. And I don't mean the type Celia would hang out in."

It's like I'm watching the innocence flow right out of her.

Her mouth pops open and closes several times.

"You...this?" she stammers. She looks from the ground, to the ceiling, to her hands and turns what might be the cutest shade of green I've ever seen on a gal. "Why are you like this?"

I look around, like she can't be possibly talking to me. "Why am I like what?"

She stamps her little foot and shoves her hands on her hips. "Males. I mean males. This is disgusting, Bren."

My wolf agrees, still, I hold my ground, growing defensive. "Don't blame me. It's not my spunk spraying the walls and ceiling—"

She gasps. "Oh, my God. It's on the ceiling?"

"I'm exaggerating." I glance up, hoping that it's just some kind of freak oil stain blurring the ceiling. "Maybe."

"Maybe?" she asks.

And there's that adorable shade of green again.

"I think I'm going to be sick," she grumbles.

I turn my head when the breeze filters through the cave and I pick up on something else.

The walls splinter, and the mounds of stone shift as something crawls beneath. "Em, we're not alone."

She turns, watching the thing snake beneath the rocks. I step forward to stay in front of her, my knuckles cracking as I tighten my fists.

"Bren," she says. "No way is it human."

She's right. Whatever it is moves in multiple serpentine motions, creating patterns that mirror the ones in the sand where Ted was murdered.

"You seeing what I'm seeing?" I mutter.

"Yes," she says. "This is what killed Ted."

"Fall back," I say. My steps are careful as I guide Emme back toward the tunnel we took to get here.

The creature advances, slipping from the mounds of stone and disappearing into the sand, the grooves it leaves behind the only evidence of its presence.

I growl, low and deep. "Emme, it's right beneath us. Get back to the tunnel, now."

Emme never gets the chance.

A hand punches through the sand at my feet, shoving me backward and slamming me into a pile of rock.

I scramble to stand. Something wide and muscular knocks my feet out from under me.

Emme screams.

And then she's gone.

Chapter Ten

Emme

Agony spikes from my ankle and stabs its way to my throat, releasing my screams. The bones in my leg snap and my foot separates at the joint.

Through the anguish, a speck of clarity pokes through.

I expect the creature to loosen its hold and slide free from the skin that's only barely keeping my foot attached. Whatever this creature is, he is strong. It's not magic pulling me through—a spell meant to drag me to the conjurer—it's something corporeal and evil; its smooth exterior cold and unrelenting.

Its latch tightens, snaking up and around my leg. I start to black out, the pain too much to take.

Push through the hurt. It's what Celia always told me. *That's how you win a fight. That's how you survive.*

My vision spins in and out, the torment so blinding, I only catch flashes of my surroundings.

Bits of light from the ceiling zoom past me and chunks of wet sand pummel my face. I'm dragged to the opposite side of another cavern, my nails breaking and my fingertips tearing open as I snatch at the sandy floor.

There's nothing to grip. I reach out with my *force*, trying to snag something—*anything*— to keep me in place. I barely touch what might be the top layer of the bubble when I'm hauled beneath the crumbling rock.

The impact stuns me with multiple punches to my face and body I can't possibly brace for.

Bren howls my name. I barely hear him. I'm buried beneath the sand, the weight pressing against my chest forcing the air from my lungs.

The mixture of stone and sand beats against me, promising me death. I can't move, the heaviness incapacitating me. I'm tugged through the rough terrain, the creature that has me reminding me that I'm not the one in control with every harsh pull.

My mouth gasps for air as I'm hauled through another pocket of space. I barely manage more than a few gulps when the painful chill of freezing water slaps my feet. I'm yanked under, into an abyss that swallows me further away and farther from Bren.

Bren. What will this thing do to him?

I kick with my good foot and flail through the frigid temperature and darkness. This thing is enjoying the ride it's taking me on. It shakes me and moves faster, incited by my suffering and terror.

The water grows colder as I'm dunked deeper, icing my bones but failing to numb the pain. The alveoli in my lungs pop in horrid bursts, caving my ribs inward as throbbing spasms eat their way through my body.

I'm consumed by it all, the fear, the injuries, the knowledge that I may never see Bren again.

Bren...God, where is he?

I lose consciousness. For a long, long time, there's only blackness until a warm bright light takes form in the horizon.

The pain vanishes and all I feel is peace.

This is it. This is death, calling me away from the darkness.

But it's not my time.

I barely think the words when a tiny flicker within me sparks into glorious light.

It wakes me with a jolt. I see it, through all the emptiness I left behind, there it is, showing me the path out.

My body explodes with pain and I'm flung like trash onto the shore.

Each cough, each sputter of water, is torturous and glorious at once. I roll onto my back and prop myself into a sitting positing, slapping at my eyes to see what exactly I'm fighting.

The fight doesn't arrive.

The limb that held me doesn't try to snatch me away.

No evil army awaits.

It's just me.

Whatever stole me away is gone. For now.

My body cannot consume enough air fast enough, nor does it stop screaming at me to lie down. But I can't lie down. I can't be vulnerable. Not if I want to live and see my family again.

My family. Do they know what's happened?

And Bren...what's happening to him?

My surroundings suggest I am in another smaller bubble. Like the one before, dark stone encases the perimeter. As disoriented as I am, I work through my thoughts, picturing how the creature that grabbed me moved. Down and across. Up. Down again. Into the water. And up once more. This entire underwater cavern is one giant labyrinth that leads to multiple pockets of air.

A shaky glance up proves I remain at the bottom of Tahoe. Instead of sand and more insects scurrying along, moonlight peeks through what feels like a mile away from the surface.

A fish swims by, and another. Neither bothering with me.

I'm okay with it. I'm not excited about joining them. There's no way I can reach the surface alone. Even if I could, I'd never make it to shore without drowning. The waves are rough, and I can barely do more than tread water. Aric taught me as much last summer. He didn't like that I didn't know how to swim. It worried him. He was always kind.

The tears I cry from the pain morph into those of a final goodbye. No matter what happens, I know Aric will take care of Celia and their little one. He won't let anything happen to them. Taran...she'll always be fine. With her verve, and Gemini there to comfort her, she'll be okay.

Shayna, my funny and carefree sister, she'll take it the hardest. Her pep is second only to her heart and the close bond we share as sisters and friends. Koda will hold her and love on her. He won't let her go, won't let her hurt alone. Eventually, she'll make it.

I wipe away my self-pity along with my tears, even though it's excruciating to do that much. I want to live. I want to see my family and Danny. And Bren.

Always Bren.

My hand presses to my side as I take a few more painful intakes of air. I've never been too hurt to heal. I am now and I need a moment.

No, it was a rough ride. I need more than a moment. I need my magic. *Breathe,* I tell myself. *Just breathe and get that air you need to focus.*

My thoughts are a spiral of emotions and ache, battering me as harshly as that creature did. It's hard to concentrate and I'm unsure I'm seeing everything I should.

I'm deep beneath Tahoe, of that much, I'm certain. Knowing so doesn't help me formulate a plan and nothing around me offers a means of escape.

There's always a way out. All the hardships my sisters and I have endured have taught me that much.

A small pool of water licks the shore, slapping gently against my heel. The water appears deeper toward the right of the enclosure where it hugs the wall. It also appears to be expanding. Every part of this labyrinth is running out of time.

And so am I.

I groan, pressing my hand tighter against my ribs when my breathing grows shallower. Goodness, I'm really beat up.

I lift my head, my eyes widening when I see what waits on the other side of the pool. Forget *my* injuries. I'm in better shape than that vampire.

His body lies flaccid on the beach opposite mine, his hips and legs partially submerged. His decapitated head teeters back and forth several feet away from his torso.

"Fuck," he moans, spitting out sand. "Fu-u-uck."

Yes, I have indeed had better nights.

My body trembles from cold and the extent of the damage it's suffered. I don't have to take stock of my injuries to recognize I belong in an ICU following the attention of several skilled surgeons. Every slight movement churns my stomach and I'm repeatedly swallowing the copious amounts of blood flooding my mouth.

My lashes flutter several times as I fight to stay awake. I'm close to fainting, again, my head having been pummeled as wickedly as the rest of me.

Keep it together, I tell myself. *You have to find Bren.*

I think I'm finally ready to heal, only to shudder violently when I catch sight of my foot. The bruising from the damaged ligaments and muscle have doubled its size and turned sections black. The actual limb lays on its side, the instep indented, and my knee and hip disconnected from their sockets.

With another breath, closed eyes, and more effort than it usually takes, I surround myself in pale yellow light, and allow my magic to begin the repairs.

A choked sob rips through my throat as my healing ability snaps my hip back into place. The soothing calm that follows enriches me and has my body begging for more. But with every trauma I heal, a jolt of pain comes. Some are worse than others, all necessary, and all rushed.

I jerk and twitch, feeling my way around each splintered bone and ruptured vessel. The creature that took me spared me from nothing. It wanted me to hurt. It wanted me to fear. And it worked.

I stare hard at my feet.

It also stirred my anger.

It takes me a long time to finish healing. I'm ready for a nap when I reach the last few fragments of bone that make up my ankle. I combat the exhaustion. As good as sleeping sounds, it will only get me killed that much faster.

The vampire's moans increase when I roll onto my knees and try to rise. "Is someone there?" he asks.

His head tilts from side to side, the slight turn he manages permitting me a better view of his face.

The bouncer, the one from the Watering Hole gapes back at me. "Food," he says through a mouthful of fangs.

He's excited to see me. I don't share the same sentiment. Without thinking, I cover my throat, very much feeling naked. "No," I tell him. "I'm Emme, not your next meal."

"Gerald," he says. He licks his lips, slicing his tongue along his exposed fangs. He laps up the blood. I try not to gag when fluid slides down and out his mangled throat. I don't do a great job. His actions pretty much sum up the fun that's made up my evening.

"Why won't you let me feed from you, Emme?"

"Do you really have to ask?" I say, doing my best to ignore him.

My legs are wobbly when I finally make it to my feet. I stumble forward with all the grace of a freshly dropped giraffe. I'm worn out from healing and the beatdown I received, and Gerald isn't helping.

"Emme," he says. "Don't be like that. Come on over and let me have a taste."

Gerald, well, back when he was whole, could have graced Parisian fashion magazines. His come-hither glance suggests he still thinks he can.

It takes more than a pretty face to win me over and Gerald's has seen better days.

"Emme," he sings. "Come play with me."

There's no sense in letting him think he stands a chance. "I don't hook up with vampires," I admit.

Despite the cold, here comes the bare beginnings of a blush. I try to hide it by giving him my back. I need to find us a way out. "What I mean is, I don't let them feed from me."

From what I understand, hooking up with a vampire is the same thing as allowing them to feed from you. Each vampire bite, suck, and swallow provide the participants an orgasmic rush. Normally, they don't require much to sate their hunger. Except normally, they're not decapitated and lying in pieces mere feet from me.

"You'll like it, Emme," he whispers. He slurps as if already tasting me. "It will make you feel good, precious."

"I'm not your precious and you need to stop," I tell him.

He doesn't, excreting more of his will.

Vampiric magic cuts through the thick layers of lust and sin coating the air. I'm not normally taken by vampire charm and the pheromones their magic emits to attract their meals have no effect on me. But this time, I can really sense it.

I fumble around the enclosure, pushing my hands against the stone. "*Abre*," I call out. "*Abre.*"

I mimic Bren's motion, as well as the extra surge of magic he released when he broke through the simple spell.

Yelling, "open," in any language would have no effect on the wards enclosing our house. They're strong. These, however, shouldn't stand a chance. They're poorly made, and yet my actions have no effect.

Several drops of water trickle against my already soaked spine. I peer up. While this bubble feels slightly stronger, like the first, it won't last.

"Emme," Gerald calls. "Come closer. We'll be friends and more my sweet."

It's comments like these that always have Taran rolling her eyes at the vampires.

I step away from the wall and walk around, putting more distance between me and Gerald. This bubble, cave, whatever this thing is, traps magic and feeds from it to maintain it. It's why my magic and Gerald's appear more pronounced. Still, there's more to this place and even more I don't understand.

My hands press against my hips as I eye up the wall, pausing when Gerald attempts to lure me to him. "I can feel you," I say.

"It's just the start, baby. I'm going to make you feel like you've never felt before."

"I mean that I've felt your magic from the start. You don't have to keep going." I shake my head. "It doesn't affect me like you might think."

"Interesting," he says. "Why don't you come over here and we'll test your theory?" He lifts his arm and motions me over. Well, that is his intent. But the way his body lies, his finger points toward the water.

"I promise, you won't regret it," he adds is if that will somehow seal the deal.

"You're old," I say. My cheeks heat when I realize how I came across. "What I mean is, you'd have to be to survive the decapitation."

"So?" he asks, rather defensively.

"It's nothing personal," I say, quickly. "It's just Misha usually permits his older vampire on his premises."

His scowl adds several points to his already creepy factor. "I'm new to the master's keep. He feels I need to prove myself." His legs kick, similar to a child at the start of a tantrum. "It's the reason I ended up here."

I remove Bren's shirt and ring it out. It's warmer outside the water. That doesn't mean it's still not cold. "I don't understand what you mean," I admit.

"If you come a little closer, I'll be happy to tell you," he promises. He makes a face when I cross my arms and fail to move. "Fine," he says. "One of those things followed you to the Watering Hole."

All right. Now he has my attention. "One of them?" I ask.

He nods, well, tries to. Mostly he just tips forward and ends up with a face full of sand. I give a little nudge with my *force* and set him back in place. He frowns. "I felt that."

"I apologize," I say. "I tried to be gentle."

"That's not what I mean," he says. "I felt your hands. From there. How'd you do that?"

"I'm telekinetic," I explain.

"No," he says. "It's more than that. I felt your touch—your fingers or something like them." He licks his lips. "I can taste you with your touch."

I thought he was trying to draw me closer. But he really doesn't know anything about me. Maybe that's what Misha wanted.

"You didn't use your hands," he clarifies.

I glance at the sand at my feet. "I don't have to. For larger objects or more precision, sometimes I do use my hands."

"What if—"

"That's enough about me," I say, trying to add some authority to my voice. "Let's talk about what's here and how we're getting out."

He doesn't reply, his grin demonstrating he's more amused than thinking twice about crossing me.

I straighten to my full height. Now is not the time to be polite. "Answer my questions," I say. "What's here? How many are there, and what do they want from me?"

He keeps his mouth shut.

I should remind him that Misha would take offense if he knew his vampires weren't cooperating with me. But this vampire, for all he wants a taste of me, recognizes the danger we're in. His features set. He knows I am his only chance at survival. "There's three of them," he says. "Freak witches from what I can tell. Two I can easily kill, *if you'd just let me have a bite.*"

Great. He's starting to fall into bloodlust. I lean forward for emphasis and to show him I'm not afraid. Regardless of his tone, I'm the one in control.

"For the last time, you can't have my blood," I tell him.

He mutters a few swears. I disregard his rather creative cursing and mull through what he says. "What about the third?"

It's only then he shows fear. "Can't win. Not alone. Too strong."

"There aren't many things a vampire can't overpower," I remind him.

"No. But I can't overpower them."

"Them?" I ask. "I thought you said two are weak and easily disposed of?"

"Yeah. I did. If only there was some sexy bombshell of a blond to nourish me."

"Oh, I see," I say. "Now I'm a bombshell. Earlier you mistook me for a teen." I sigh. "Tell me about the third witch. Was she the one who sent that creature after me?"

He laughs without humor and more than a little hysterically. "Honey, she didn't send that creature after you, she was the creature."

"She's a shifter?" I say, fearing the worse.

Shifters are witches who spend decades making blood sacrifices to their dark deities. In exchange they receive the power to change into any animal alive or dead and carry the power of hell within them. If this witch is now a shifter, Gerald is right, we can't kill her alone.

"I wish." Gerald cuts himself off when he realizes what he said. "Never mind, I take it back."

Something hits against the opposite wall, causing the bubble to shudder. The pool expands and deepens, drawing closer to my feet.

"Shit," Gerald says. "This whole place is going to blow soon."

A glance at the ceiling assures me he's right. A miniscule hole pokes through the ceiling, dripping water in the center of the pool. Tahoe is a pure source of magic. Whatever darkness these witches have managed to manifest beneath it won't last against Tahoe's power.

"Tell me more about the witches," I say.

"Which one?" he asks. He rolls his eyes. "The smaller two aren't right. The other one, the big one is worse, scary worst. These witches fucked up the laws of nature trying to prove a point."

"And what point was that?" I ask.

He meets my face, unblinking. "That despite how weak their magic is, together they can be just as terrifying as anything out there."

"They're Lesser witches with something to prove?" I surmise. He nods. "I don't understand. They already proved their strength against the necromancer."

"Not these Lessers, Emme. The Lessers you speak of wanted to be something and made something of themselves. They stayed in school and learned. They didn't get kicked out on their asses and asked never to return."

I think back to the bodies Shayna and Koda are investigating. "They're Lessers who never graduated or developed their magic," I reason.

"Duds," Gerald agrees. "Their power was piddly at best. That didn't stop them from wanting what their brethren had, the clout, the prestige, a coven." He spits on the ground, or at least tries to. "They formed their own family and went after everything they felt was owed to them, including vengeance."

"Vengeance against whom, exactly?" I ask.

He laughs, his voice echoing in the small area. "Anyone and everyone who ever told them they were nothing."

"While I don't agree, I can understand their bitterness," I say. "But what does that have to do with me?"

"I don't know. All I know is the mousy one was after you." He shrugs, although it looks odd when a body without a head does it. "The master told me to keep you safe. I did. Look at where it landed me."

Gerald slaps his hands against the beach when the pool reaches his shoulders. He pushes up on his arms and suddenly stops moving.

I turn in the direction of his darting eyes. "You want to know what all this has to do with you?" he asks.

My hands spread out at my sides as the magic builds along the wall. "They're coming, aren't they?" I ask.

"No," Gerald says. "They're already here."

Chapter Eleven

Emme

A small section of cave dissolves. It's unlike when Bren pressed his weight and said, "*Abre*." The walls don't crawl away and create a larger opening. This is different. A fissure creates in the structure and parts like a heavy curtain, allowing two women hooded in worn gray cloaks through. As soon as they pass, the opening closes behind them.

The first witch is petite, like me, only malnourished. I can tell by the way the cloak clings to her small, hunched frame. Her hands curl deep within the sleeves as if she's cold. The second witch follows closely, shuffling her feet. She should lead, I think. She's taller and while as underfed as the first, she's physically more imposing.

Like Gerald, I already know I can fight them alone. They're neither formidable nor healthy. They're sick. My healing touch senses their worsening states as they approach. I'm uncertain what's happened exactly but their bodies are turning against them. I can feel it.

With their hoods as long as they are, their faces are obscured and their vision limited. But when I do catch my first glance, I wish I hadn't.

Long black whiskers poke out on either side of a little pink nose encased in white and copper fur. She pauses almost in front of me and whips back her hood.

"You're alive," she squeaks. And I do mean "squeaks."

"Ah," I answer.

Gerald described her as "mousey." He should have said she is actually a mouse.

The fur around her eyes and nose are white, the rest of her, including her fuzzy ears are copper. And her hands? Those same hands I thought she huddled deep in her sleeves because she was cold. They're not hands. They're shriveled paws.

She would be cute. If she wasn't so creepy!

I should lift her and her friend into the air. I should smash both of them against the rock wall and quickly kill them. Taran would.

But I just can't.

She turns to her friend. "What are we going to do, Farrah?" she asks. "I can't kill her, and I won't hurt her."

Farrah whips back her hood. "You're asking me, Merche? I didn't sign up for any of this."

Not to be mean, but I can honestly say Merche is the better looking of the two. Where Merche is a mouse (possibly a guinea pig?), Farrah is a fish!

The rest of Farrah's body is human and possibly naked under that cloak. Her head is that of a blowfish. She doesn't have fins, and honestly, that's the only blessing. Large bulging eyes blink back at me and pulsating gills make up her ears. Her head inflates and deflates as her extra-large, fish lips, take in copious puffs of air.

The fact that they don't attack and are hesitant to hurt me keeps me in place. "What do you want from me?" I ask. "And what did you do with Bren?"

They jolt, surprised it seems that I can actually speak.

"The wolf you were with?" Merche asks. "He's okay. Well, no. He's very angry."

When Farrah rolls her fish eyes, it darn near tops the list of disturbing things I've seen tonight. "Angry is an understatement. He's pissed-off and tearing the cell you were last in apart."

Bren's safe. For the moment. That doesn't lessen my fury.

My voice steals, and for once in my life, whatever these bad guys catch in my features is enough to make them back away. "What do you want from me?" I demand. They attempt to scramble away. I follow. "I'm not going to ask you again."

"You're cute when you're mad."

"Shut up, Gerald," I snap.

I fix my steely gaze on Farrah the fish and Merche the mammal. Forgive me, it's the only way I can remember who's who.

Merche steps forward. "We didn't mean for this to happen," she says.

"You didn't mean for what to happen?" I ask. Frustration heats my face. I lift my arms to motion around but also in preparation to strike if I must. I pity them. They're scared and in a ton of trouble. That doesn't mean I'm not ready to protect myself. "Tell me what's happening and I may spare your lives."

And...they both start crying.

I made a guinea pig and fish cry. Perhaps on my way home, I should find a puppy to kick.

No. Scratch that. I love puppies.

"Tell me," I say, keeping my voice stern.

Merche wrings her small furry paws and exchanges several glances with Farrah. "What other choice do we have?" she asks her.

"Can we get on with this shit?" Gerald very helpfully interjects.

"It started out as a good thing," Merche squeaks.

"A great thing," Farrah adds, nodding in a way that makes her face flop back and forth.

Oh, goodness. I almost gag.

"I don't give a damn how it started," Gerald says. "We want to know what the fuck we're doing here, and we want to know now."

"That's enough out of you, Gerald." I face the witches. "If you want me to help you, you need to help us. Start from the beginning and make it fast."

I cross my arms, hoping to appear more threatening. The walls shudder and shift, a stark reminder that our time is limited and we need to move quickly.

"I'm from New York," Merche says. She points to Farrah. "Farrah is from Boston. We didn't um, we didn't graduate from school." She glances down, her long whiskers twitching. "Like the rest of us, we were actually asked to leave."

"There's more of you?" I ask. I don't want to think about what other crossbreeds are lurking around the labyrinth. But I would be a fool not to ask.

"No," Farrah says. "Just Una."

"Una?" I ask. "Your leader?"

Merche fiddles nervously with her whiskers. "She is now. But she wasn't at first." Thick tears run down her long nose. "You don't know what it's like to be a witch and never really become one. You embarrass your family and ultimately they shun you. If you're lucky, you'll end up in a carnival reading cards and telling fortunes the rest of your life."

"And if you're not?" I ask when she grows silent.

"You end up here," Farrah says.

She breaks down, her face inflating and deflating with each harsh sob. I can't even watch. Neither can Gerald. His body crawls toward him and his hands lift his head to turn it away.

"Where is here, exactly?"

"It was sold to us as the Promised Land," Merche says. She cleans off the tears from her fur that continue to fall. "We were going to have our own coven, our own place to belong where we could roam with other supernaturals. At first, it was nice to be around more of our kind. But then the other witches, still weaker, but stronger than us, realized just how many we were, and thought we could do more as one."

Farrah begins to pace, her face inflating and deflating with each step. I cover my mouth, hoping to mask my retching.

"We started working on developing our skills," Farrah says. "It was like witch school only slower so we could keep up and work on our strengths."

"That sounds appropriate," I say, carefully. "What went wrong exactly?"

"Everything," Merche says. "It didn't work. Our improvement was minimal at best. As a result, the higher ups started experimenting with stronger spells, just to try to give us an advantage."

"But there was only one spell that really worked," Farrah admits, ignoring my blatant horror.

My hands fall away from my face. "Oh, no. You cast Mirror."

They regard me as if slapped by one of Farrah's missing fins. "How do you know about Mirror?" Merche asks.

Farrah seems disturbed. Never mind, I think that's just how the poor thing looks. Mirror isn't a spell I'm supposed to be familiar with. Even Lesser witches are banned from knowing about it.

They don't understand that there's a great deal I've learned about magic and a lot more I don't care to know. Each class of supernatural are bound by loyalty to protect their secrets. As a non-witch, and someone who doesn't belong to a coven, I'm not bound to these rules and explain the extent of my familiarity with their spells.

"Mirror is one of the three High Tasks of Witchcraft. Casting one successfully is your final exam and what permits you to graduate."

"That's right," Farrah says, her large bulgy eyes watching me closely.

"If performed correctly, the spell-wielder turns into someone or something else."

"Who told you about Mirror?" Merche asks.

"That's not important," I say. I examine them closely. Their forms are only portions of what they should be. They also seem comfortable in their bodies, as if they've occupied them for a while now.

"This doesn't make sense," I say.

"We're not lying, miss," Farrah assures me.

"What I mean is, Mirror is an espionage spell. One meant to last only a few hours, a day on rare occasions. You've been like this for some time now, haven't you?"

Merche nods.

I groan and put some space between us when I realize what's happening. "You didn't perform mirror. You couldn't have." *You were too weak.* "They, your so-called leaders, performed it on you."

Farrah looks down, mumbling as if merely speaking aloud and doing her best to justify her actions. "We had to try other ways. We had to experiment. It was the only way we were ever going to make something of ourselves."

"That's not true," I say. "It's what your leaders told you to get what they wanted from you. They were terrible, selfish people."

"They weren't all bad," Merche insists, crying faster. "Some were good and wanted better for us. Except the others killed them until they were the only ones left."

"They?" I ask. "You said only Una was left."

Merche is crying so hard she can barely speak. "They're *all* Una. They combined and became one."

I'm supposed to face my enemies with a poker face. If they don't know what I'm thinking, they can't anticipate my moves. I stay safe. I maintain control.

Maybe, in another few decades or so, I'll master that ability instead of allowing every emotion I'm feeling to play across my face like a symphony.

Horror, disgust, and fear drain the warmth from my skin. I'm clutching my heart and bouncing back and forth. In my defense, I don't run around in circles screaming like I very much want to.

"Okay," I say. "How do I fit in? Why am I here?"

"You don't want to know," Merche says over Farrah's, "We never wanted to hurt you."

I lose what remains of my patience and freeze in place. "I want to know, and regardless of what you say, you very much hurt me."

"Una told me to follow you," Merche says, quickly, her nose twitching. "She found you tonight at the wolf's house."

"First date," I interrupt. I hold up my hand. "Very much not my boyfriend."

"Oh, we know," Merche says.

I don't question how they know, but it still strikes me as strange.

Merche blows out a breath. "Just so you're aware, Una ripped him to pieces."

"I know," I say. "We found the body. But why?"

An odd look overtakes Merche's vermin appearance. "Una can be very beautiful when she wants to be. She enjoys sex. We all do." She clears her throat. "Your lover seemed to as well."

"She lured him to the beach to have sex with him and then kill him?" I ask.

They both nod as if it's the most normal thing in the world. "It's how we feed Una and make our money. We bring lovers back here with the promise of sex for a price."

"Do you keep those promises?" Gerald asks, a little too enthusiastically.

"Yes," Merche says. She shrugs. "It's the only way we're allowed to get close to anyone and the only way Una receives satisfaction and nourishment."

"And men willingly come here?" I ask. "With you?" I grimace. "Um. Sorry, I didn't mean for it to come out like that."

"Yes, you did," Gerald says.

Yes, I did.

Merche smiles sadly. "We know what we look like, and we know what we've become. The men came with us before the results of Mirror fully kicked in," she replies. "Now that we look the way we look, there's no men and no more money."

"And no food," Farrah adds. "We haven't eaten real food in a long time. Except maybe worms and scraps. They aren't as bad as you might think."

"Mm," I say. "Una eats her lovers?" Again, more nods. "Is she a praying mantis of sorts?"

"Oh," Farrah says. "That is one of the Mirror creatures she initially used." She pokes Merche. "That explains a lot."

It occurs to me then why these witches never developed their skills. Both are very naive and don't strike me as overtly intelligent.

"Tell me more about Ted and Una," I say.

"Who?" Farrah asks.

"Emme's boyfriend," Gerald offers.

"The wolf I went out with tonight," I clarify.

"Oh, him," Farrah says. She kneels at the edge of the pool and dunks her head into the water. Bubbles form along the surface. After several long and disturbing seconds, she lifts her head and splashes more water along her scales.

"Better?" Merche asks.

"Ya," Farrah says. She rises slowly. "In another few days, I don't think I'll be able to leave the water."

"Can we get back to Ted?" I interrupt.

Farrah glances at me, her body appearing more apologetic than her fish face. "Una didn't want anyone around who might protect you. She wants you dead. Needs you dead, actually."

It's only because she says, "need," that I start to understand. "Because of my power and who I know."

"Yes," Merche says. "If you're not around and Una manages to hurt your pregnant sister, you won't be able to save her. The Mate and her baby will die, and the dark ones will finally respect Una."

Chapter Twelve

Emme

It takes a while for me to move. Rage has a funny way of keeping me in place. How dare she? How dare they?

"They won't go after Celia."

"She's well protected by the wolf and his pack," Farrah agrees. "But Una has a plan—"

"You don't understand," I snap. "She won't go after Celia because I won't allow it." I permit my protective streak to come forward and vanquish that guilt that frequently haunts me, the one attached to blood and death. "My sister and her baby are going to live. No matter what I have to do, they will share a lifetime together. Every mother and child deserve as much."

Merche shakes her head. "You don't understand Una. She's strong, vicious, as if all the wrongness from our strongest brethren collected into one being."

"I don't care. Whatever Una is, she won't be enough," I tell them. "I'll kill her before she can think of attacking Celia."

Neither appear to believe my words or think I have it in me. That's their problem. Not mine.

"What's her weakness?" I ask.

Merche averts her chin. "She doesn't really have one," she mumbles.

"Yes, she does," I disagree. "Her magic is pathetic at best if she's nothing alone. What else? We all have weaknesses. Tell me something I can use, and I may be able to help you out of this mess."

Farrah splashes more water on her face and hurries to me. She motions to her features, her movements excited and hopeful. She might be smiling. Never mind, she found a worm to munch on.

"You can help us?" she asks between slurps. "You know magic—magic that can reverse all this?"

I watch what's left of the worm disappear into her mouth. *Not even a little bit, girlfriends.*

"No," I confess. "But Genevieve does."

My words are meant to reassure them that I'm an asset and that I can help. That's not how they take it. They cower. It's then I notice Merche's tail. She tucks it between her legs and backs away from me.

"She knows Tahoe's Head Witch," Merche squeaks to Farrah. "And she calls her by her first name."

"*She* can hear you," I say. "And, yes, I know Genevieve."

"And she knows you, too?" Farrah presses. "You didn't just meet her in passing?"

"Genevieve very much knows who I am," I reply.

My relationship with Genevieve was always cordial. She respects us, especially Celia. But I'm neither a witch who reports to her nor someone required to grovel to win her favor. For the first time, I realize exactly how much other witches esteem and fear her.

"She's actually very nice," I add, trying to soothe their unease. I give it some thought when I take another gander at their, um, conditions. "To me."

Farrah tugs on Merche's sleeve. "The great Genevieve will kill us. She has to for the crimes we've committed."

"Not necessarily," I claim.

I'm starting to lose them and work to steady my voice. "The witches, especially Genevieve, are part of our alliance, and we're part of theirs." I ease closer to them with my hands out. "If you help me, if you do all you can to get me out of this situation, I'll speak to her on your behalf."

"But you're no one," Farrah says. "You're just the sister of the Mate who carries the Chosen One."

Warmth encases every part of me, and despite the cold, you could likely grill a steak on my face. I straighten, allowing my anger to dissolve my passivity and give me the mettle I require. "If I was no one, you wouldn't have a need for me, would you?" I ask. "But I am someone."

Farrah rolls her eyes. "Who?"

All right. Now I'm mad. "*I* am the healer of the Wird sisters. *I* have the power to soothe and cause pain." I clench my teeth. "And *I'm* the one who can crush you without ever lifting a hand."

I use my *force* and give them a small shove to prove my point. My anger and desire to prove myself makes me a bit aggressive. They land on their tails, well, Merche, I mean. Farrah face-plants into the water. In my defense, I think she rather enjoys it.

It takes all that I have not to apologize and hurry to help them back to their feet. It's hard to be kickass when my nature is to be kind.

I shove aside my gentler disposition, reminding myself this is not the time for compassion, and take several deliberate steps toward them. "I'll speak to Genevieve, not as the pack alpha's sister-in-law or the sister of the Mate, but as the friend and colleague the Head Witch of the Lake Tahoe Region has grown to admire."

They jump when I point to the vampire. I almost jump too, stunned by their reaction. I clear my throat. "What about him?" I demand. "Why is he here?"

"He spotted me waiting for you," Merche says. "Una sent me to hex your phone so you couldn't call for help." She stands slowly, careful to avoid facing me directly. "We were to wait for you to leave the bar and follow you. Once you got to the highway, Una had planned to take you."

Merche assumed I'd be alone. "You didn't expect me to be with anyone?"

"You're never with anyone," Farrah says. Her face remains under water and bubbles balloon and pop along the surface with every word. "At most, we would have to get rid of the Uber driver."

Wow. To them, I was merely this lonely and pathetic young woman they needed to snag. It's why they presumed Ted wasn't my boyfriend.

Merche continues, unaware of the insult. "The vampire came after me. He would've killed me if I hadn't made it to the beach and summoned Una."

Gerald's decapitated body huffs. "What did you expect?" he demands. "The master told me to kill anyone who tried to hurt the Wird Girls."

"The master?" Merche squeaks.

Gerald laughs, his chest moving up and down while the sound echoes from his mouth. "Yeah, bitches. *The master.* You not only went after Aric Connor's sister-in-law, you targeted a friend—wait, you are just a friend, right, Emme?"

"Yes," I say, worried where Gerald's headed with this.

"You're not doing the master, are you?"

This time, I'm the one squeaking. "I have *never* been intimate with Misha."

"She calls the master vampire by his first name, too," Farrah bubbles out.

"Oh. Must be the other one," Gerald reasons out lout. "Either way, you girls are fucked. You took me, and you took one of the women my master swore to protect."

"This is why you're here," Merche squeaks to Gerald. She swipes away angry tears. "You couldn't keep quiet." She lifts her little nose, her attention returning to me. "When the vampire told Una you were under his protection, it infuriated her."

I take in Gerald's debilitated state once more. "I can see that," I agree. I think matters through. "But why didn't Una just kill him like she did Ted?"

Bubbles spume under water as Farrah explains. "Oh, because Una needs to eat," she casually offers. "She tore Ted apart to feast, but then had to drop his pieces to save Merche from the vampire. The other *weres* arrived before she could return to consume her meal."

Merche plays with her little paws. "Una had to disable the vampire so he wouldn't cause trouble. He's to make up for the nourishment she was supposed to receive eating Ted."

Gerald's hands lift Gerald's head off the ground. "Wait a minute. I'm here so she can eat me?"

"And I'm a pawn to be disposed of," I bite out. My glare trains on my captors. "Una didn't care if I suffered. From the moment she formed her plan, she counted on my death. It guaranteed I could no longer heal and protect Celia, as well as offered a demonstration of her supposed strength." I shake my head. "It's sickening. All this to win evil's favor and hurt someone I deeply love."

"I don't want to be eaten," Gerald interjects.

Shame hunches Merche's small frame. "We didn't want you to die, Emme. We didn't want anyone to die. All we wanted was a place to belong."

"There are better ways to find your tribe," I tell them.

"Not for us," Merche replies.

I cross my arms, tired of their excuses. "Why didn't Una kill me outright? Why did she just toss me here and leave?"

Farrah lifts her head from the water. "Una thought you were dead, we all did," she tells me. Like me, she's ignoring Gerald's mounting hysterics. "She told us she felt your soul leave your body."

I did, too.

The realization is almost too much to bear. I huddle into myself. Had my magic not fought to keep me alive, I wouldn't be standing here now.

Una, like everyone else, underestimated me and my power. For once, the lack of faith worked to my advantage.

"I eat others," Gerald says. "Get it? Others *do not* eat me."

"Una will be here soon," Merche says. She fumbles with her paws as she looks around. "We're supposed to nourish the vampire so he'll regenerate and provide her a better feed."

I pivot away from them. "Fine," I say. "You do that."

"What?" Merche says.

"Huh?" Gerald asks.

"Gerald, you need to eat. You'll get better, and then you can fight." I whirl, making a point to meet each witch in the face. "Then we're finding Bren and getting out of here."

Tears pour from Merche's beady eyes, soaking her fuzzy features. "You don't understand, we can no longer find our way out. We're trapped in here just as you are." She looks at Farrah, her squeaks more terrified. "And Una...Una will kill us if we help you in any way."

Farrah's face expands and deflates in quickening motions. "I don't want to hear your excuses," I say before Farrah can argue. "You're already dead. You just don't know it yet."

Merche loses her composure, crying loudly. I don't hold her little paw or gently stroke the fur on her head. I don't even try to slick back the scales sticking out near Farrah's gills. We're past tenderness and sympathy. Only survival remains.

"Mirror took a long time to work on you," I remind them. "Now that it's begun, it's manipulating the magic inside you in the way that it shouldn't. There are reasons these High Tasks are assigned to witches close to the end of their studies. You're beginning to see what happens when such a powerful spell goes wrong."

"Our friends are dead, Merche," Farrah blurts out.

"Your friends?" I ask.

They both nod, but only Farrah replies, wetness releasing from her bulging eyes. "Their bodies couldn't handle Mirror."

"Is that what Una told you?" I ask.

This time, when they face me, they see the truth they've for too long suppressed. I continue, knowing they don't want to hear it but also recognizing that they must. "Mirror didn't kill your friends. Una did. Their bodies were found tonight, all dismantled like Ted and in varying stages of decomposition."

A new form of sadness takes over Merche's disposition. "Did they look human? Or did they look like us?"

"Human," I say. Shayna and Koda would have told me otherwise. "My guess is the spell broke with their passing." I ease away from them. I've never had to share news of this magnitude and force the words out. "This spell is changing you into something you were never meant to be. You're sick and your condition is worsening. I can sense it with my magic. It's not just food you lack. Your animal counterpart is fighting the human side that remains."

"Is the animal trying to kill us?" Merche asks.

"At the very least, it's attempting to dominate you," I explain. I've spent enough time with *weres* to understand as much. "It wants to live just as much as you do."

Farrah grips Merche's hand as she addresses me. "But you can help us, right? You won't let us keep turning, will you?"

"I'll speak to Genevieve," I promise. "If anyone can reverse or dissolve the spell, she can."

"What about me?" Gerald calls. "Still hungry and decapitated over here."

Even ignoring Gerald is a chore. I do my best, keeping my full attention on the witches. "The choice is yours," I say. "You either help us and have a chance at life, or you die along with Una." My voice tightens. "I won't spare anyone who steps in my way."

I walk away like a boss.

Or at least I try to.

"I'll feed him," Farrah says, a little to anxiously. "It's been a long time since I got some."

My feet stumble to a halt. "Got some?" I repeat. I understand what she means. I'm just dumbfounded someone in her state would be so brazen. I can smell the illness ravaging her body and I can sense it with my *touch*.

"Yes," Farrah says. "Do you really think anyone would want me like this?"

"That's not how I meant it," I reply.

"Then why are you looking at me that way?" she asks. She smooths the scales closest to
her gills. "I may have fish parts—"

"Ew," Gerald interrupts.

Farrah shoots Gerald what may or not be a dirty look. My apologies. With Farrah, it's hard to tell.

Farrah continues although it's clear she didn't enjoy the interruption. "Like I was saying, we may have fish parts, but we're still females with needs." She stops herself when she realizes she referred to herself in the plural sense. "We want and need sex. We enjoy that sensation of ache and delight." She grows defensive when I don't respond. "Haven't you ever had an orgasm, Emme? Don't you revel in them?"

"I'm not discussing my private life with you," I reply. The realization of what's happened slows my response. Mirror's damaging effects reduced intercourse to a primal level, impairing her human mind and clouding her judgment. I doubt Farrah would be so blunt under better circumstances.

No wonder the Lessers engaged in sex for money so willingly and recklessly. Their animal counterparts don't require the love or commitment I would. Fish engage in sex for the sake of procreation. To them, it's a part of life. The same, I presume, applies to mice.

The witches surrendered to the desires of their animal counterpart. Just like Una surrendered to her predatory nature.

"You won't tell me about your sex life because we're not friends," Farrah reasons.

She appears confused that I'm not as open as she. "It's personal," I reply, hoping to leave it at that.

Farrah's fish lips open and close as if trying to form words. I think she means to argue. Instead she flaps her gills, whips off her robe and...

Oh, my. I was right. The rest of her is human and very naked.

Gerald positions his head on his shoulders, salivating at Farrah's approach. But it takes him ramming his eyes shut before he takes that first bite.

Like the crunch of bone, he digs in. Farrah straddles him, her protuberant eyes rolling like marbles.

Merche removes her robe, her beady eyes shiny with desire as she watches Gerald feed.

I back away, jerking when the water stirs and Bren breaks through the surface.

Chapter Thirteen

Emme

Bren doesn't run to me.

He charges.

In one smooth move, he leaps from the water and yanks me to him, his soaking wet clothes clinging to him as he presses me into his hard body.

A growl unlike I've never heard from him punches every syllable. "Are you okay?" he asks. "Are you hurt?"

I hug him tight. *He's okay. He's safe. He's alive.*

"I'm fine," I stammer.

His voice is more animal than man. "I don't believe you—"

He hauls me behind him.

"What the hell is this shit?" he demands. "Is that vamp fucking a fish?"

"Um," I say.

Okay, where to begin.

Bren backs us away. "Holy shit. He is fucking a fish."

"Gerald is actually just feeding," I explain.

Bren doesn't believe me, and why would he? Farrah's eyes are spinning, her gills and lips cyclically flapping.

"What the hell is going on here?" Bren roars. His jaw pops open when Merche pokes her head around a large pile of broken rock. "Emme, is that a goddamn hamster?"

Merche gives a little wave with her paw, her whiskers twitching anxiously. "I, um, no," I reply. "Actually, I think she might be a guinea pig."

Bren is not in his happy place. He reels on me. "I leave you alone for fifteen fucking seconds and this is the shit I find you in? Fish girl and leech boy going at it—"

Gerald stops feeding just to yell at him. "I need to eat, man."

"—and a naked mouse with hooters watching the show," Bren snarls. "This is some PT Barnum freak show, Emme. We're getting out of here, *now*. Guardian of the Earth or not, I draw the line at this bullshit. Christ, I thought you were dead."

He reaches for me, only to freeze when my eyes sting. I specifically told myself I wouldn't cry, except here I am. With Bren this close, with him being exactly how he is, protective, mouthy, and fierce, it's like I can cry, I can release those feelings I pushed aside.

He's right. I almost died. Somehow, I lived and now he's with me.

Fear replaces the anger sharpening his features. "Jesus," he says, clutching me against him. "That thing, it hurt you, didn't it?"

All I can do is nod.

Bren stiffens. "How bad?"

I release a breath. "Pretty bad," I admit.

I wipe away my tears and look up at him. "There's a lot you need to know, and we don't

have much time. That thing that grabbed me, she's still out there and she's coming for all of us."

Fury shadows his face. "All right," he says. "Let's talk."

He takes my hand and leads me as far away from Farrah and Gerald as we can manage. It's hard to find a place to stand. In the short time that's passed, the pool has expanded significantly and there's not much left of the beach.

I speak fast, telling Bren all I know, including my plan.

"I don't know about this, Em," Bren mutters. "I say we ditch the fugly mutants and find a way out on our own." He winks at Merche when she looks up at him. "How's it going, fuzz face?"

Merche wrinkles her nose at him, her whiskers all a flutter. "I think she'll prefer it if you call her Merche," I tell him.

Bren grimaces when Gerald steps away from Farrah and Merche throws off her cloak and scrambles to him. Merche exposes her neck, offering herself eagerly. I expect jealousy from Farrah but she barely notices. She throws herself into the pool and starts doing laps, eager to cool her flushed skin.

Drops of Tahoe's water land on my head. A new pinhole has formed in the ceiling.

"Damn it," Bren mutters. "This whole place is coming undone."

He lifts me and places me on an incline where the sand is less moist. It's strange. He could have just asked me to move. He didn't have to touch or move me as he did.

"Bren, I realize your hesitant to align with the others and that you're anxious to leave. I am, too," I whisper. "But I'm not certain we can find our way out without some help and I'm less certain we can take Una on without them."

Bren rubs his jaw, considering our choices. "Em, all this is not what I expected," he says. "Except while I don't trust them, I do trust you. We'll try it your way."

"Flounder," he calls. "*Hey.* Flounder."

"It's Farrah," I say, speaking low.

Farrah stops swimming. Her body remains very much post-coitus red despite the non-intercourse and despite the cold water. "You talkin' to me?" she asks.

"You got it, fish face."

"*Bren,*" I admonish. "That's awful."

He throws out a hand. "Come on, Em. It's not like this gal doesn't know she has gills." He looks at Farrah. "You do know about the gills, right, Nemo?"

If fish could freeze someone with one look, Bren would be a popsicle. "Yes, wolf," she snaps.

Bren continues, unaffected by the dirty looks and the way her googly eyes spin with annoyance. "If this bubble pops, or if my girl Emme here finds herself under water, you're in charge of getting her to safety." He points at her. "That means land. She can't swim and if she drowns, you're the one I'm coming after."

"I don't respond well to threats," Farrah fires back.

A sense of ire encompasses Bren, warming the frigid air encasing us. He takes a step forward. Farrah stumbles away from Bren and all but scales the wall. "It's not a threat, Dory. It's a promise. *You* got yourself into this shit. *You will* get the person helping you out of it."

Farrah nods, or at least tries to. Farrah doesn't really have a neck.

Bren returns to his place at my side, rolling his eyes when Gerald and Merche resume their very audible exchange. "Damn. It's like tuning into some twisted Discovery channel documentary. You sure they're not fucking?"

I glance around Bren's super-sized body. All of Merche's limbs are flailing as Gerald sucks and pulls at the skin along her throat. "No, just feeding." I tilt my head. "Can't you see them from here?"

"Emme, it's not that I can't see them, it's that I don't want to like, ever," Bren tells me flatly. "This shit is messed up two times past Tuesday. If I look, I'll puke. Do you know how bad it has to be for a werewolf to puke?" He hooks a thumb behind him. "That bad."

I'll admit, that is pretty bad.

He bows his head low enough to drip water from his wavy hair. "Look, I need you to know something, all right?" He meets my gaze. "If anything happens to me, I wouldn't feel right if I didn't tell you."

You like me? Please say that you like me.

I reach for his hands and hold them carefully, surprised that I find myself smiling.

Bren doesn't smile, his entire demeanor reflecting his sadness.

"Em," he says.

And then nothing more.

I stroke his hands gently, waiting patiently for him to form his words. It's a sweet moment, lovely. Perfect with the exception of all the gobbling Gerald is engaging in.

Gerald lifts his head briefly, spitting out fur before resuming his meal. Merche doesn't seem to notice. She's caught up in the moment, and all the pleasure she derives from having a vampire feed from her.

"Just tell me, Bren," I say. The way he takes me in borders on magical. He's never looked at me this way before. "You can tell me anything. You always could."

He works his jaw, his disposition changing the more he takes me in. My body swells with warmth. Bren does like me. And it's more than just as a friend.

I'm ready to tell him how I feel. He doesn't let me, speaking quickly. "I tried to break out of that area we were in," he says. "I beat at the walls and smashed through a few layers. Except all the damage I did led to more walls. That thing, whatever took you, it was too hard to track."

I loosen my grip to his hands, doubting whether I read him correctly. "Then how did you find me?" I ask.

Bren's broad chest heaves in and out. "My wolf," he says. "He latched onto your presence and led me to you."

I tilt my chin. This wasn't what I expected. "I thought you could only track by scent?"

He shrugs, appearing nervous. "I did, too. Except, you know, it's not like you're some stranger whose aroma I have to figure out or distinguish from the other gazillion smells out there. I don't have to get a sense of you like, I would a perp I'm assigned to track. You're Emme. My, you know, buddy."

"Oh." I release his hands. "That makes sense."

Bren starts to walk off, appearing restless, but almost immediately returns. "This whole place is like one giant maze, even under the layer we're standing on. There are dozens, if not hundreds of passageways beneath us. I think it's how the creature has survived Tahoe's magic so long, it tried to burrow into the lake floor and distance itself from the water where the magic is more potent. The thing is, the lake found a way through anyway, it's why the whole structure is disintegrating as fast as it is."

"Oh," I say, realizing how much worse everything is.

"The passageways the creature took you through were too narrow for my wolf. I had to swim through them in human form. It's why it took me so long to find you. I kept popping up in the wrong spots. Good in a way because I was able to get air, but bad because you weren't there."

"It's all right," I say, recognizing how bad he feels. "I used the time to figure things out and formulate a plan."

He strokes my damp hair. "Yeah. You did good, Em."

My eyes widen as Bren releases a bone-rattling growl. I turn toward the water, the sense of evil and wrongness returning with a vengeance. "It's Una," I say. I back away from the water's edge. "She's coming."

Chapter Fourteen

Emme

Bren snarls. He senses Una's arrival, too. And he's not alone.

Gerald releases Merche, spitting out chunks of fur as he jets to our side. His head flips flops from side to side, harsh enough for each ear to alternate hitting his shoulders. The witches may have provided him enough of a feed to reattach his head and seal the skin, but not enough to repair the vertebrae.

"The crazy bitch is almost here," Gerald tells us.

Oh, yes, she is.

The water charges with magic, lighting up the pool in a wash of green and blue sparkles that reflect along the wall.

"Tahoe doesn't like her," Bren mutters. "All that is the lake's magic is fighting hers."

Merche and Farrah clutch each other, racing away from the water's edge. Bren's focus bounces from them to the pool. "Hell, it doesn't like you either."

"It's because the magic they used for Mirror was just as dark as what made Una," I whisper.

The pool spills over and splashes against our feet, bubbling as if boiling. I barely register what's happening when Bren drags me behind him. "It's banging the crap out of Oompa's magic."

"Una," I remind him. I lead him to where the witches are hugging the wall. "Do you think Tahoe can kill her?"

"Yeah, I do, but not quicker than she can get to us," Bren says. "Tahoe's packed with enough good magic to suffocate the bad. But it's like I said, she's kept a safe distance from it by burrowing underground. It'll be hours, or maybe days before Tahoe breaks that freak apart, and that's only if she stays underwater long enough, which she won't do. She's too smart."

He whistles, trying to snag Merche's attention. "Mickey, hey Mickey. Get us the hell out of here."

Merche doesn't take too kindly to the mouse reference. I think she tries to flip Bren off with her paw except it doesn't quite work due to her lack of fingers.

"Come on, Merche, go," Farrah urges. "We have to at least try to find our way through the tunnels."

Merche adjusts her position beside Farrah and they begin their chant. I don't understand enough Latin to interpret what they're saying, but I recognize enough words to know they repeat the spell more than once.

The wall beside Gerald starts to split and a section breaks off and lands in the water. "Any day now, ladies," Bren calls behind him.

"We're trying," Merche squeaks. "But it's like you told us. Tahoe doesn't like Una or us. It's blocking our spells."

"Try harder," Bren snaps.

The opposite wall cracks. Bren presses his body against me, shielding me from the crumbling rock. Gerald is beside himself, jumping in place and causing the sides of his head to slam repeatedly against his shoulders. "I don't want to die," he says. "No way, not like this. Not under the damn water like a punk, and not after I sucked a fish."

"I can respect that," Bren agrees. "How we doing, witches?"

"We got it," Farrah calls.

A crackling noise accompanies a break in the stone. It opens enough to allow Merche through.

Farrah doesn't stand a chance. Bren lugs me away in the opposite direction as an octopus tentacle thrusts though the water and snatches Farrah by the waist.

Farrah screams.

So does Merche.

So do I.

So does Gerald.

"An octopus," Bren says, pointing. "I fucking knew it."

He shoves me in the direction of the fissure as Farrah is forced underwater. The horrible sound of shattering bones precedes Farrah's reappearance. She floats to the surface of the water, belly up, her lifeless protruding eyes no longer moving.

Bren urges me through the opening. "Go, *go*."

The rock edge scrapes my shoulders and rakes at my shirt as I angle my way through. Gerald is a tighter fit and Bren barely makes it through.

I move forward blind, using my *force* to feel around the tight space. It's better than using my hands but not efficient enough to run.

"Bren," I call out. "I can't see."

"I've got you, Em," he yells. "Harold, go after the mouse."

Gerald doesn't bother to correct his name. "On, it," he says.

Like a spider, Gerald scrambles up the wall and onto the ceiling, passing over top of me.

The stretch of space we're in widens enough to allow Bren ahead of me. He clasps my hand, hurrying us ahead.

A collision of rock and magic shake the ground at our feet. "Mother fucker," Gerald hisses.

He's somewhere to our far left. But it doesn't make sense, there's only wall and stone. He screams, the agony in his tone paining my ears.

And then he's gone.

I clasp my hand over my mouth. "Oh, Gerald," I say.

"Yeah," Bren mutters. "It must've been his time. But it's not ours, Em. This way."

We dash in the opposite direction we heard Gerald cry out. We're farther along and pass into another cell. This one is more of a cave. Stalactites in varying length and width hang from the ceiling.

I'm out of breath from running and breathing in the stagnant air from such an enclosed space. "Do you think we're closer to the surface?"

Bren takes a sniff and curses. "No. These aren't mineral deposits like in caves. It's the same crap that makes up the wall."

He presses his hand against my shoulder, driving me backward. I think he hears Una, until the walls splinter and crack. A large stalactite falls, and another. We double-back, returning to the small pathway as the opening of the cell we were just in collapses.

The sound of rushing water fills my ears and the cavern floor grows wet and cold. Panic threatens to consume me. We're in a dark maze, filling with water, and no exits in sight.

"Bren," I say.

"Don't," he tells me. "I'm going to get you out of here. I swear to God I will."

Merche's squeaks reverberate from further away and down toward the right. She's in pain, and she's scared, each sound sharpening to an ear-rupturing squeal.

The entire area shifts forward at an angle and we fall, the frigid water soaking my chest and legs and threating to split my bones.

Merche shrieks and shrieks, her terror adding to mine. I cover my ears, but I cannot muffle her torment.

Merche and Farrah were wrong to do what they did. But they didn't deserve such a harsh end. I promised to help them if they helped me.

I promised!

Bren clasps my wrists and gently pulls them down. "Emme, we have to keep moving," Bren tells me. "Come on, baby. There's nothing we can do for her now."

A harsh wave knocks me down when I try to stand.

Merche stops screaming.

Except for the increasing rush of water, there's only silence.

Bren lifts me, steadying me when another wave strikes us and leaves us in waist-high water.

"We have to go back," he says. He positions himself in front of me, moving us through the freezing enclosure as fast my feet will allow.

My teeth are rattling so hard, dull pressure builds along my jaw and head. I stir my healing *touch* awake, beating back the hypothermia setting in.

We cut left and then right, the rising water bites across my shoulders.

"I can't *change* in here," Bren tells me. "There's not enough space. But if this place fills up with water, grab onto my neck. You hear me? I'll get us back to where we were."

I don't question his tactics or ask him what we'll do if that cell is gone, too. Bren's fighting to get us out. I won't distract him with stupid questions or blatant fear. Even if this fear is unlike any I've ever felt.

Bren rounds another corner and we force ourselves up an incline. The entire labyrinth has reformed. If it weren't for his sense of direction and ability to reverse our steps, we would have perished where we last heard Merche.

"Do you think Merche is dead?" I ask.

"The mouse?" he asks. "I don't know. She sounded hurt and this place is falling down around us. It doesn't look good for her, Em. The vamp? I'm guessing that thing definitely found him."

"If so, I can't imagine he survived her," I say.

"If it came down to a fight, probably not in his condition. 'Cept it's hard to tell anything in here for sure. Everything echoes in these tunnels and I lost track of him when he went after the mouse. All I know is that we're on our own and we have to get out before that thing tracks us down."

My body is trembling out of control when we finally reach the other cell. The shift in the wall caused the opening to widen, but it also allowed more water into the small space.

Farrah is gone and the pool has flooded the area in waist-deep water. Bren lifts me and places me on a section of stone wide enough to stand. He looks around for something he can work with, but there's nothing. Just rock and water and sand.

I glance up at the clear ceiling when he does. A school of fish jet by, frightened and eager to escape from something more vicious and larger.

"She's out there," Bren says.

I nod and grip the side of the wall for balance when that touch of evil spirals into a storm of terror. "I can feel her. She's coming." I start to climb down. "Should we hide?"

He shakes his head. "No. She knows we're here, just like she knows we're trapped. I can get us to the surface, Emme. But I'm not sure we'll make it before she sees us, and no way will she just let us swim to shore." He meets me square in the face. "We're going to have to fight our way out."

In the water.

In the deep.

Where I can't swim.

I don't blink. "All right," I say. "Let's do this."

My head shoots up and Una appears.

Una isn't exactly an octopus. She's a nightmare. Given our current situation, I'd prefer an octopus. In fact, I'd prefer an entire octopus consortium wielding knives and machine guns.

Every other limb that stretches out before us holds the hand of a different witch. One is sickly yellow like the underbelly of Una's suction covered skin, another is a grisly pink to match the color of her exterior. The two that remain are darker, one a deep olive, and the last like spoiled milk chocolate.

I don't remember a hand touching me when she initially dragged me into the cell. It must have been one of her four tentacled limbs. They're longer than that of a regular octopus, a combination of cephalopod and human parts.

"Aw, hell," Bren mutters.

He's watching her bounce along the ceiling, practically mesmerized. It's understandable. Una is grotesquely beautiful, the manner in which she moves reminiscent of a bride lifting her gown to dance.

Except Una isn't the blushing June bride. She's evil and dangerous, her dexterity and unique style of locomotion adding to her lethality.

She pauses as if suddenly noticing us, stretching her limbs and adjusting her gangly frame to peer down at us.

"Oh," I groan over Bren's very audible, "fuck me."

The faces of the witches who make up the creature that is Una merged into one. Four sets of eyes stacked into rows blink back at me from the top of her large forehead. She doesn't have a nose, but she does have several chins crowning her lower jaw. She smiles with her large mouth, giving us a good view of the rows of dagger teeth stacked on top of one another.

"We should have hid," Bren says. He cracks his knuckles as he takes another good look at Una. "Yup. Definitely should have ran away like bitches and hid from this shit."

He starts to back away. He doesn't quite reach me when a tentacle punctures through the bubble and slams Bren into the opposite wall, pinning him.

I jump into the water and splash toward him, shoving the first hand that reaches for me away with my *force*.

Uma's limb feels heavy as well as strong. She's also absurdly fast.

My hands shoot out as I slap the next limb away. The rejection angers Una, she clicks her fangs, her gestures and whale like sounds, pulsating through the air.

"Go, Emme," Bren yells. "Yes!"

The dodging, the scooting, and the hammering I avoid must look pretty kick-ass from Bren's perspective. He believes me agile and that I'm averting the mighty villain's blows.

Good. Let him think that. Let *her* think that. Mostly, I'm retaliating blindly and stumbling through the water and unsteady floor.

The walls have crumbled into large sections of rock that poke out from the bottom in varying sizes. They slice at my skin and clothes. I use my senses, pushing my *force* out when I feel her approach and move as fast as my environment permits.

I'm almost to Bren when a suction covered limb adheres to my waist and cocoons my body.

The pruney hand at the tip tightens around my throat, releasing me briefly just to belt me across the cheek like an impudent child.

I wince from the pain. The slap is hard enough to leave a mark, but not enough to cause serious damage.

I was ready for Una this time and used my *force* like a shield. Pale yellow light envelopes me as I put some space between her limbs and my body. It's not enough to move. Just enough to safeguard my bones and organs and allow me to breathe.

Water cascades on me like a waterfall as Una lifts me away from Bren. To her, I'm nothing, just a broken doll to play with as she wishes.

Well, she has another thing coming.

Water sloshes through the bubbled ceiling as Una slithers her way in. The magic she used to create the shield holds enough to allow her through without completely dismantling its protection. But her grand entrance did fill the cell significantly more.

What remains of our exit is now fully submerged. It doesn't matter. This isn't the way we're leaving. I glance at the ceiling.

The moonlight that poked through earlier seems further away. I hope Bren's right. I hope he's capable of swimming to the surface.

"What are you looking at, my dear?"

With her back to me, I think Una is talking to Bren, until she gives me a little shake.

"Our way out," I reply.

She laughs. I didn't think Una could get any creepier, but here she goes, proving me wrong with her caw-like giggles. "You think you're getting out?" she asks.

I try to shrug, but her hold is too tight. "No. I know we are."

Taran always talks a big game. Like Taran, I'm counting I have the goods to back it up. "After I reduce you to slivers," I add.

Una stills. So, does Bren. Like me, they cannot believe what just flew out of my mouth.

"Heh, heh," Bren says. "Damn, girlfriend. You are one ugly bitch."

He's trying to keep Una's attention on himself instead of me. One hard squeeze. That's all it will take for Una to kill me. My *force* is just a temporary fix. I can't hold off Una forever. If I don't break this hold, she'll crush every part of me, starting with my larynx.

Una reels on me. I would have startled had I the space. Bren's right. There are cuter scoundrels in the world.

"We know what we are, wolf," Una says. Foam spills from her mouth as she speaks. Another hand appears and strokes my hair. "We're not like the pretty, pretty, Emme. Are we?"

"Keep your fucking hands off her," he growls.

"We don't want to," Una coos at me.

Hers face blurs and twists into that of an Asian woman, to an African American, and then back to two more Caucasian women before resuming her gruesome appearance. "You caused us much trouble tonight, little one," Una says. "We don't like trouble." She gives another squeeze, smiling when she senses my power hold. "Unless we're the ones to cause it."

Una drops me. I hit the water hard and go completely under. Bren's roars beat through the rush of water and the ache that reclaims my muscles. I paddle to the surface, gasping from the cold and lack of air when Una lifts me again.

This time, she has me by the ankle. The same one she broke the first time.

I dangle several feet from the water, spinning and spewing everything I swallowed. I try to gather my bearings. It's not easy. Once more, Una is in total control and reminding me as much.

The difference this time is I don't need to know exactly where I am. I only need to know how far away the floor is where those sharp sections of broken rock await.

I get a feel for the distance and attempt to reach out. Una shakes me like a dog would a squirrel the moment she senses my magic. I clear the nauseas effects of the harsh motions by coughing, barely catching sight of Bren when another limb snakes around me and Una rights me midair.

It's only then I see just how bad things are.

Bren's head is knocked repeatedly into the wall as two other limbs pummel him. His face is badly bruised, each attempt his wolf makes to heal him, interrupted by more blows.

His demeanor is more beast than human. He's close to *changing*. Una knows as much and tightens her hold. To *change*, Bren will have to bust a few ribs. Based on the ire overtaking him, he's ready to take that risk.

"You didn't think I was a threat," I yell to Una.

My voice trembles as badly as my body. Am I angry? No. I'm livid. And I'm just getting started.

Una turns her distorted head. One blur of motion follows the rest as a multitude of faces poke through her rubbery exterior, demanding attention and fighting for control.

With each stretch and twist in her features, the portions of broken skin and missing muscle grow more pronounced. Tahoe is breaking Una apart as we suspected.

It's up to me and Bren to give our beautiful lake the help it needs to finish.

"Oh, oh, oh, oh." Her squawks change in pitch, depending on which face dominates. "She challenges us. We don't like being challenged."

Her wet limbs slap against the stone walls, holding her position to better angle her body in my direction.

"But she makes us laugh," Una says. She forces out a giggle to prove her point. "Such a small piddly thing believing herself so grand."

I steel my nerve, refusing to let her intimidate me, although she very much does. "You don't think I can hurt you," I say.

No," she admits. She sounds bored. "Not like the others." The face with the multiple eyes returns in time for her to laugh again. "You move things. Large things sometimes. But that's not enough. What hurts us is we can't hurt your sister. Not with you around to help her mend."

She shakes her head, allowing the face of one the Caucasian witches to make a brief appearance. "The healing, small person. That's what we must rid ourselves of. That's what we hate. We can't kill the Mate and her spawn. No, no, no. Not with you around."

Bren's growls shake the ceiling, allowing more glacial water to spout in different sections. It rains down on me in sheets, icing over my already wintry skin.

All right. Enough of this.

I peg Bren with a look that tells him it's time. His nod is barely perceptible, but it's there, and it's all I need to act.

"You think my healing ability is my biggest threat?" I ask.

Una froths at the mouth, anxious to take a bite. "What else do you have?"

I smile. "The ability to shred you apart."

In a holler of rage, my *force* unleashes, sending jagged fragments of stone from the sandy floor soaring upward. They strike in a brutal wave, slitting Una's skin and hacking into her underbelly. She screams as dissected chunks of flesh pelt the air.

Bren and I remain safe, cocooned in her tentacles and protected from the sharp fragments slashing Una apart.

Her hold loosens.

But I'm not done.

My gaze latches onto her face. In one unsparing move, my *touch* extracts her eyes from their sockets.

Chapter Fifteen

Bren

The winter before my best friend, Danny, became a werewolf he caught the flu. I didn't know what the hell to do with him. Snot was coming out of all sorts of places I didn't know existed. It was nasty. I couldn't deal with it.

Emme couldn't heal him. She can't heal any illnesses. But she knew exactly what to do. She brought over homemade chicken soup. She changed his sheets. She covered him with a soft blanket she knitted just for him. She made sure he had enough to eat and that he drank plenty of water. She took care of business.

Just like she's doing now.

The eyes she wrenches from Octobitch's head fly in all directions, except for one. As the Puss loses her grip, I kick away from the wall.

I launch forward, catching Emme as she falls and curling my body into hers. With a wicked splash we land in the water along with the rocks Emme used as weapons.

My ass and back take a beating as I stroke like a banshee to get us to the other side. It's not pretty and hurts like hell.

And it's worth it. I spare Emme from all of it.

We surface near sections of stacked stone. I shove Emme toward a pile that should hold. She reaches for the ledge. I reach for her ass, pushing her up.

Una whips about, flailing and searching for us as ink pours from her face and damaged limbs. "What did one sheep herder say to the other?" I ask.

Emme turns. "What?" she asks.

"Let's get the flock outta here."

There's that smile and determination I love. She climbs as fast as her small frame allows.

Except, I shouldn't have said jack. Una may be blind, but she's not deaf. Her head wrenches in my direction. I leap, *changing* into my wolf and scurrying up the wall.

Emme has barely climbed more than a few feet. She stops and shoots her hand out, her teeth gleaming as she clamps them down.

I don't see what Emme sees until severed limbs slap the space near my hind legs. I launch off the wall, using the weight of my six-hundred-pound beast to slam down on Una's head.

I'm back in the damn water, and Una doesn't want to let go. I chew and rake through the remains of two limbs before I break free and resurface.

Swimming is one of my strengths. But the force of the water busting through the ceiling is almost more than my beast can take.

The cell is filling fast. I'm trying to keep pace with all the crashing waves triggered by the influx of water and Una's spasmatic movements. I scramble out of her reach each time she nears, but only just barely.

It takes some muscle and speed to put enough space between us. I swim in a zigzag pattern to avoid those freak hands. With the motion of the lake and all the debris I'm trying to avoid, I struggle to reach what remains of the wall.

My paws dig into the rock. It brittles beneath my weight and almost right away, I'm back in the water. I try again, fighting for each stride I make, all while checking to make sure Emme hasn't fallen.

Waves splash against my tail. I'm making headway, just not fast enough. This place will cave inward in one shot and it's filling faster than we planned.

I jerk my head up, hoping like hell Emme still has room to breathe.

Pure fucking joy has me wagging my tail when I find Emme cowering in a small groove within the wall.

"*Bren*," she says.

I can't tell if she's crying or if she's just wet. It doesn't damn well matter. I've never been so happy to see this pretty face.

She clutches my neck, her slender arms giving warmth and love all at once. "You're here," she stammers.

Jesus. Her lips are blue, her skin is the color of my ass, and she's shaking out of control. I *change* to speak to her, wishing to heaven and back I could just hold her.

"Time to go, baby," I tell her. "You ready?"

She glances up to what remains of the translucent shield, her gaze targeting a hole just big enough for two. "Not really," she admits.

I smile. Or at least try to. "Neither am I, but I say we haul ass anyway."

She chokes back a sob and a laugh, the way she does when she knows we're absolutely screwed and scared out of her mind, but somehow still believes we'll make it anyway.

I *change* back to wolf. The moment I feel Emme settle onto my back I take one last leap of faith.

Together we bust through what remains of the ceiling. And hell, has kicking ass never felt so right.

I'm no longer swimming. I'm propelling myself to the surface like a shark ready to maul anything that gets in my way.

Emme's little. That means she has little lungs. The pressure of moving this fast could burst them, 'cept drowning will kill her just as fast.

Hang in there, Em. Don't you give up on me.

My hind legs pump hard, fighting against the instinct to slow and permit my wolf's essence to finish healing me.

Emme's hold loosens and her body starts to float away just as we break through the water.

I *change*, wrenching her into my arms.

The moon basks us under the best damn light I've ever seen and I'm holding the best girl I know.

"Yeah," I holler. "We made it, baby!"

Emme coughs and swipes at her face several times. She blinks away the droplets coating her thick lashes and throws her arms around me.

The shore, it's not too far away, and the docks are only a short swim away at best. I should start swimming, get her to land and safely back home.

Like a jackass, I don't move. I tread water and just look at her, smiling till my face actually hurts.

"Bren," she says, holding me close. "I can't believe, I mean, goodness. I can't believe we did it."

"No, baby," I say. "*You* did it."

The smile she greets me with should be illegal. I maintain my position, taking her all in beneath the moonlight's haunting glow.

It's been a crappola of a night. Dawn isn't far away, and neither are the docks. Still, I don't move, stealing more time with just me and Emme.

Her angelic face grows sweeter as she adjusts her position. For the first time in my life, I know there'll never be a woman this beautiful. I lean in, ready to kiss her.

Emme jerks her chin away, panic overtaking her in one vicious strike. Sparkles of blue and green flicker from the bottom of the lake, growing in size, and spreading in cahoots with that sense of evil.

"Bren! Una's still alive."

I roll my eyes. "Yup."

Emme screams when I throw her up and away from me. With a large intake of air I howl, summoning the pack with my *call*.

A long tentacle grapples my waist. This time, I don't let it tighten before I *change*.

My fangs tear through the limb pulling me under. Una, shrieks, her mutilated form, slinking away. I dive after her, needing her carcass floating over Tahoe more than I need my next breath.

I'm almost to the crazy witch when she spins like a top, belting me with the stumps of her remaining tentacles. She sucker-punches me in the chin, stunning me long enough to engulf me with her shredded extremities.

Una tightens her vice-like grip, squeezing out the measly amount of oxygen I have left. I curl into a ball and kick out, puncturing her injuries with my claws.

I fight, snapping my fangs and pummeling her with my limbs. But it takes me biting off most of her face for her to finally release me.

I jostle away from her, the lack of air circulating through my blood making me loopy and robbing me of my speed. With all the grace of a toddler, I reach the surface, spitting out water and hacking up Una chunks.

My head whips in the direction of the Watering Hole when the *weres* I summoned race toward the dock. From the entrance to the labyrinth, the *weres* from the apartment complex hustle in beast form, their paws kicking sand behind them. To the west, more *weres* approach in a boat. They're coming. All the packmates out on patrol are answering my *call*.

But I don't need them.

I need Emme.

Relief warms the chill from the lake and I just about collapse when the fish gal lifts Emme from the water and up to a large dock. The tide must have dragged Emme farther down and away from where I aimed.

Mouse girl tries to reach for Emme with those tiny-ass paws, but it's the vamp with the twisted head who places Emme safely on the dock.

My lungs are on fire and my body is trying to realign at least three busted bones. I'm tired and famished. But I keep paddling with my tongue lolling out, happy as wolf who caught his prey and anxious to be with my girl.

Shit.

My girl?

Here I go again.

The closer I draw to Emme, the colder she appears.

No. Not cold.

Emme is *pissed*.

She snaps a large branch from a nearby tree with her *force* and levitates it into the air.

"What the hell?" I ask.

The *weres* on the dock and fish girl frantically point, yelling all at once. I turn slowly as it occurs to me, no one is actually looking at me.

And I swear, it's like the theme from *Jaws* starts playing.

Una's head pops to the surface like a fin and she charges. She can barely see with that one eye dangling from her skull. But she sees enough.

And so does Emme.

Like an arrow meeting a bullseye, Emme nails Una in her large head with the branch. The sharp tip splits her head open. She wobbles back and forth and sinks.

As the last of her vanishes beneath the water, she loses her fight against Tahoe.

Una detonates. What remains are pieces, swallowed whole by the lake.

"Oh," I say, turning back to Emme. "I thought you were mad at me."

Rain trickles across the water, dimming the rising sun and rushing the moon away. I hurry to the dock. Someone throws a blanket over Emme, but it's not enough. She needs to get out of those wet clothes and wash leftover Una bits off. She needs food and warmth.

Hell, she needs me.

The bear from the complex passes her the phone. "It's the alpha, Aric Connor," he tells her.

Emme grips the phone tight, taking a moment before speaking. I hurry forward, only for Houndstooth jacket and the Polo boys from the Watering Hole to shove their way forward.

"What the hell was that, man?" Orange Polo asks. "A wereoctopus?"

"No. It was something else," I answer.

I scowl when the cougar from the complex adjusts the blanket covering Emme's shoulders. She's talking to Shayna. I recognize Shayna's excited tone right away.

"Sure was something else," Houndstooth agrees. He jerks his head in the direction of the fish and mouse. "Just like them."

The cougar nods, his hardening gaze fixing on the younger *weres*. "When you talk to Bren Cooper, you call him alpha. Show some respect, dawg."

The other *weres* nod in agreement, eyeing fish girl and the president of the mouse club with disgust. The witches didn't cast Mirror under the laws and safety of their coven, and they're not *weres* or humans our *weres* are obliged to protect. They're abominations, results from the evil we guard against. If left on their own, the fish and mouse would be eviscerated by the pack.

"What do you want me to do with them, alpha?" the bear asks.

In other words, kill them now, or later?

"Don't know," I say. "Still waiting to hear."

I take the beach towel he offers me and wipe down. The witches inch away from the *weres* and closer to Emme. She's talking to Shayna now. I recognize the perk to her tone. A hiss from a werelynx warns the witches against getting too close to Emme.

"You promised to speak to Genevieve," mouse girls calls to Emme. "You said if we helped you, you would help us." She veers on me. "Emme was drowning. Farrah dove into the water and brought her to the dock."

"It's true. The current was carrying her away," fish girl replies.

Fish face looks up at me hopefully, her bulging eyes spinning with worry. Like the rest of us, she took a beating. I can't believe she made it out and I gotta give her props for helping Emme.

"Is the Head Witch nice, like Emme says, wolf?" she asks me. "Do you think the Great Genevieve will spare us?"

"Are you kidding?" I reply. "Genevieve's a bitch. She'll skin you alive and use your hide for dinner napkins."

Emme gasps. "Bren!" She speaks through her teeth. "I'm on the phone with her now *and she can hear you.*"

"Oh." I scratch my beard. "Waddup, girlfriend?" I ask into the phone.

"Burn in hell, mongrel," Genevieve replies.

Like always, Genevieve keeps her voice calm and maintains her composure. I chuckle and finish drying off. I have to give it to Genevieve. I only saw her lose her shit once. It was all Taran's fault and it was fuckin' glorious.

Emme turns away, apologizing for my "actions, crass, and rudeness." I don't get it. I asked how she was doing.

When their conversation ends, Emme's features soften and she addresses the witches. "The *weres* are to escort you to the Head Witch's compound. There, you'll be granted an audience with her and her council."

"But will she kill us?" the mouse squeaks.

Emme isn't one to lie. She also isn't one to offer false hope. "Genevieve is not pleased with your actions, but she's willing to hear your side. I explained how you helped us, for that she is thankful." She smiles. "So is my brother-in-law, Aric. He promised to speak to Genevieve on your behalf."

The mouse addresses the vampire. "What about you? Did you tell your master how we helped you and Emme?"

The vamp scoffs. "Hell no. The master doesn't care."

I make a face. "He really doesn't," I agree.

Man, Emme is seriously cute, even when she's shooting us dirty looks and all but smacking us upside the head. She pauses as she catches everything south of my waist, blushing when she sees me notice.

I do her a solid and tie the towel around my waist. She clears her throat, after another glance my way and speaks quietly to the witches. "I will talk to Misha as well. But it's Genevieve you're obliged to meet with first." She hands the cougar back his phone. "My brother-in-law, Miakoda Lightfoot, and my sister, his mate, Shayna, will meet you and the witches outside Genevieve's compound. They're en route now. I apologize, but my family are the only ones permitted onto the premises. Are you available to take Farrah and Merche?"

The cougar grins. "Anything for you," he says.

Anything for you, I repeat in my head. *Asshole.*

I shove my way between them, grinning all the while baring my teeth. It's a rare talent. Feel free to envy me at any time.

I clasp his shoulder, hard enough to almost knock him to the ground. "Looks like you have everything squared away. Great job." I clamp down again when he starts to rise, making a point to pretend to look around. "Good job team. Way to be heroes."

The *weres* collectively nod and grunt, seemingly proud and feeling good about themselves. You know who can hype up a crowd? This guy. Right here.

I sling my arm around Emme and lead her toward the walkway, pulling her close when the breeze pics up and she shivers. "Are Shayna and Koda coming for you after they're done at Vieve's? Or do you need me to take you back to your place?"

Emme pauses at the end of the dock. She lifts her chin to better see me, her demeanor changing from someone who's had one hell of a night to someone who doesn't want her night to end.

"I don't want to go home to my family," she tells me. "Bren...I want to go home with you."

Chapter Sixteen

Bren

I know that look. I see it all the time at the end of last call. It usually comes from a *were* who was eyeing me up all night, or on a rare occasion, a human who isn't put off by the beast within me.

I've *never* seen that look on Emme.

But tonight, I really want to.

Without thinking, I tuck her close against me, just like I would that *were* or woman who wants me.

No.

That's a goddamn lie.

I ease my hold. Emme is my friend. That sweet gal I've known for years. The timid one who's fine walking behind her sisters so she never has to lead.

It's not that Emme doesn't have it in her to charge into battle, or that, like her sisters, she hates that supernatural spotlight that follows them everywhere she goes. It just has everything to do with who she is.

Emme is comfortable in her own skin. She doesn't need attention, despite the males knocking each other in the skulls ready to give it to her.

Emme...she just needs to be her. It's why I've always liked her. And maybe why I hope I'm reading her right.

Celia is the leader, the protector, the first of the sisters to go balls in with Taran running and swearing at her heels.

Shayna? Damn. For all her perkiness that cheerleader will stake your ass as quick as she flashes a smile. For someone who skips into danger, Shayna is damn scary.

Emme just wants them to be okay. She wants everyone to be okay. She's the heart, the light, the one who embraces kindness as she would an abandoned kitten left to die on the street.

Shit. This can't be happening between me and her.

She's just a kid.

She was always just a kid.

I march ahead, keeping my attention on the lamppost that starts flickering out, and the one after that.

"You cold?" I mumble, wanting to know when I lost my ability to enunciate.

"Yes," she answers.

"You're hungry, too. Right?"

"Yes," she answers slowly. I feel her looking up at me. I don't bother to return the favor.

"I suppose you want to get clean and dry?"

"Um. Yes?"

I turn onto the next block, no longer afraid and maybe more than a lot relieved.

Okay. Yeah. She just wants to wash up and get into some clean clothes. That's all it is, numb nuts. Save that horny crap for the ladies back at the Hole.

My hand drags along my hair. It's still soaked like Emme's. No wonder the poor kid wants to get inside and warm up. Hell, it's still another ten-minute walk to my place then another twenty by car back to her house.

"I think Heidi might have some stuff at my place," I say.

"Heidi?" she asks. "You're thinking about Heidi? Now?"

"Yeah," I say, wondering why Emme looks so surprised. "She used to leave a lot of clothes behind when she started dating Dan. I'll hook you up."

"Oh. Of course," she says. "Thank you."

Like a moron, I make the mistake of looking at her. The makeup she wore, if she wore any at all, was washed clean in the water. Her eyes, face, and full lips, every part of her carries a tinge of blue. She should be miserable, bordering on psychotic. But here she is, beaming.

Aw, hell. That smile she gives me, it's like, I don't know, like no one else exists. Except we're just going to my place just to hang out, to get dry, and definitely not have sex.

No sex.

Not for this guy.

Not for me.

Not for Emme.

Sex. I had to go and say it.

Now, that's all I can think of.

And I'm thinking about it with Emme.

There are dumbasses, and then there's me. All I see is her, spread across my bed, her back arching just so when I—

"Are you all right with taking me home?"

I'm ready to tell her no. That it's a bad idea. That she's better off strolling into a frat house naked with a trayful of cookies and a beer keg strapped to her back. But then she crinkles her nose in that adorable way and, and, and, *blushes*, and I know that I'm done for.

"Oh, *hell* no."

Her cheeks go from soft pink to I'm-on-fire crimson. "Did you just say no?"

Another blush, another confused yet adorable look, another sparkle across her eyes. Damn. What guy stands a chance with her? I'm only half-human after all.

"It's just crowded there," I yell for absolutely no reason. "You feel me? Not a lot of room with all the furniture."

"What furniture?" she asks, looking at me like the imbecile I am.

"The couch and TV and the bed."

I stop at "bed."

Like, stop dead at "bed."

Everything I'm telling her is a total lie. I have a decent-sized place. And with what I make between the pack and the bar, I don't need a roommate.

Right now, all I need is Emme.

Emme being Emme, does her best to believe me. I mean, why would I, Bren, her friend, lie to her? Still, she's been to my place plenty of times and can't understand why I'm telling her what I am.

"Um. Are you worried Danny and Heidi might be there?" she asks.

I can't keep up with the lies and feel worse that I'm lying to such an honest soul. "No," I mutter. "He moved in with her a while back."

She angles her chin to better see me. "Then why don't you want me to come home with you?"

Because no way in hell will I not try to sleep with you.

"Bren?" she asks. "What's wrong?"

"We almost died tonight," I bite out.

Instead of easing away, she leans into me, slipping her arm around me and partially covering me with her blanket. "I know," she says gently.

"And it's late. You haven't slept."

She motions to the rising sun and how it's working to break through the overcast sky. "Actually, it's very early."

It is. Cold and dark for a morning in July, but still early like she says.

The rain drizzles to a stop along the main road. The Hole is only another block away. It comes into view slowly, a lone soldier standing among the silence.

Man. The entire area is deserted, giving it a feel of twilight instead of breaking dawn. In almost every apartment building we pass, the lights are off and there's no speck of motion. I take a sniff. This isn't the first time it's rained. The weather must have kept enough people indoors and away from the danger. Those who hit the clubs are now long tucked in their beds or someone else's. Except for me and Emme.

Me and Emme.

Here I go yet again.

A car drives by, the opened windows giving me a hint of what's inside. Instead of taking more of Emme in, I focus on those scents. The driver didn't bother with a shower when he left his house. He skipped out for the donuts. A dozen fresh and glazed sit in a flimsy cardboard box beside him, a bag of bagels, closer to the dirty carpeted floor. They intermix with an old aroma of spilled beer.

Another truck follows shortly after that, the cabin reeking of rust, gasoline, and lawn clippings. Those two vehicles make the only sound with the exceptions of a few birds that have begun to chirp and Emme's bare feet lightly slapping against the concrete.

Emme healed enough of her injuries and is trying to match my stride, to walk along with me, to be *with me*. I forge ahead, trying to leave her behind. Without me, she's safe. She won't get hurt, and I won't make her cry.

"Is everything okay?" she asks.

Nope. Not even a little bit.

Emme is decent. She doesn't belong with a wolf like me. She doesn't need the tears I would cause. Nah. Emme deserves better than that.

She gasps, struggling to keep up with me. "Bren," she says. "Why are you running?"

I'm trying to tire you out, dammit, so you can just crash in Danny's bed and not, *definitely not* in mine. "Just stretching my legs, Emme," I say like a douche. "Come on, it's good for you."

"D-don't you think we had enough exercise for the night?" she stammers.

She sounds winded. Nice. If she had Celia's endurance, I'd be screwed. That tigress can go for miles without breaking a sweat.

Emme catches up to me and circles my waist when we reach the intersection. Stupid Do Not Cross signal. I could have made it and further worn her out.

As the sign changes, she adjusts the blanket and grabs my hand. I frown. What the hell does she use on her skin? She feels like silk. Did she have to go and feel this good?

Emme is breathing hard. I slow enough to let her catch her breath. Her labored respirations combined with the warmth her close contact brings only makes me think of her lying naked beside me.

My mind wanders to yet another place I shouldn't go. Where could I touch her to make her breathe like that for me, and how will the rest of her silky skin feel rubbing against mine—

Aw, man. I'm ready to kick my own ass.

We're standing in front of my apartment building when I realize I don't have my stupid key.

For all that running I made her do, Emme doesn't seem any warmer. She shudders, bouncing in place, the concrete at her feet doing nothing to keep her warm. I can't let her keep suffering like this. It's time to wolf and man up.

"*Fine*," I grumble, giving in. Emme is coming into my apartment. She's going to shower and get warm. She's going to have some food, take a nap, and then I'm taking her home. That's it. No fooling around.

"Fine?" she asks.

"Yeah," I say, resolution steeling my voice. "Hang on."

She squeals when I toss her over my shoulder. I rush through the alley and leap onto the fire escape.

I usually leave my windows unlocked and sometimes opened. Anyone would have to be naive or suicidal to break into a werewolf's apartment.

We reach the third floor in no time flat. I place her down and throw open the window to my living room. The motion drops the towel wrapped around my waist.

Emme's focus drifts down. It's brief, her head snapping up the moment she realizes I notice. Her large, beautiful eyes and her guilty expression give away the attention she gave Little Bren, and the longer I eye her, the more embarrassed she appears. Her lips remain blue and her messy hair is mashed against her face and scalp. God help me, there isn't anyone prettier out there.

The clouds return full force, battling it out with the overcast sky, and beating back what little sun had blurred out the gray. Rain as cold as the first frost pelts us in large drops, wetting down the patches of dry skin our bodies managed on the walk here.

It's raining a-fuckin-gain. We're getting soaked and colder.

And none of it stands a chance against this unfamiliar heat between me and Emme.

What the hell is happening? Emme has been my pal for years. Where was the shift? *Was it* in Malaysia when that fool chased her down? Or when that witch tried to gut me?

The clouds bust open and rain pours. Neither of us move. I have to get us inside. I know this. But it's like I can't and don't want to move. This moment, right here on the cold metal fire escape, can't end. It's perfect. Right and wrong at once. Sweet and sinful at the same time. Pretty in all the ugly.

Finally, I move. Finally, I speak. Logic somewhat winning out.

"Shrinkage," I say.

"Huh?"

It's what she says, except when she looks past my waist, she knows. "It shrinks when it's cold," I add.

Like my ass is on fire, I hop up on the sill and crawl through the window.

Chapter Seventeen

Emme

Bren holds out his arms and lifts me through the window. He sets me down like I would an art piece made entirely of glass. Without another word, he shuts the window to the living room and crosses the room into his bedroom. Instead of following him, I stand where he left me and try not to drool.

"Fine ass."

That's what Taran would say.

"Bren has a fine ass."

I've seen Bren naked plenty of times. When you have *weres* for friends, it's inevitable. But I've never really looked at him naked before. In the past, I've tried to respect his privacy. Now, I'm positively gawking.

Bren re-enters the room carrying fresh towels and a flannel shirt.

"I can't find any of Heidi's things you can use," he says. "Just bathing suits and a couple of old Halloween costumes." He holds out a hand. "Don't ask. Me and Dan, we don't go there."

It's all white noise. Bren is still naked, not that he has anything to be embarrassed about. That T-build, those muscles, and the eight-pack of abs are hard to ignore.

I do my best and focus on his forehead.

He rubs his head, appearing confused. "Blood?" he asks.

"What?"

"You're looking at my forehead, Emme. Did I get cut up or something?"

"You're fine." *Don't look down, don't look down, do not look...oh...my.*

"How about a shower?" he asks.

"Yes," I reply, a little too eagerly.

"Em? You all right? No offense, but I'm thinking you're coming down with hypothermia. Get a hot shower and take some time to heal yourself. You can use Danny's bathroom. It's cleaner than mine."

Bren drops the towels and shirt in my arms and leads me into Danny's suite. As he bends to start the water, I have to cover my mouth to keep my tongue from lolling to the tiled floor.

"I'll shower too and fix some grub. You want some?"

"Yes," I rasp.

Bren lifts his head slowly and glances at me over his shoulder. He looks scared and possibly thinking I'm brain damaged from the fight.

"Tea," I answer quickly. "Tea would be lovely."

My response satisfies him enough to leave me unattended. I watch him exit the bathroom, angling my body to steal one last look at him before he shuts the door tight.

I can't keep my eyes off him.

I step into the shower and try to focus on healing my injuries and the damaging effects of almost drowning (twice!).

On the dock, I only tended to my most pressing injuries. There wasn't time for all the scattered and throbbing bruises claiming my muscles or for the burning cuts that sliced my scalp and skin. I needed to be well enough to speak to my family, and of course to Genevieve.

The hot water allows me to relax and simply breathe. Beneath the spray, the stress disappears, permitting my *touch* to pass along my beaten form and alleviate my pain.

It doesn't take long. It also doesn't take long for my thoughts to return to Bren.

As I lather my skin with soap, I wonder what it would feel like for Bren's rough hands to pass along my body. Would his strength be brutal and sweet in all the best ways? Or would my very presence cause him to turn away.

His rejection would cast the last bitter slap. Just as his attention would vanquish all the hurt and terror that pummeled us.

The more I fantasize about being with Bren, the more I desire it as my reality.

The worst he could do is say no. It would embarrass me, but it wouldn't end our friendship. We've known each for so long, after all. And sometimes friends can become the best lovers.

I climb out of the shower and dry off, pausing with the towel pressed against my chest. I made my decision.

I'm going to make love to Bren.

A swipe at the mirror reveals my post-fight face. The hot shower returned the pink tones to my cheeks and lips. A little lip gloss would help and maybe a swipe or two of mascara. But my purse with all its contents was lost, as well as my shoes.

It doesn't matter. We survived, even when we thought we wouldn't. Right now, I feel the best that I will ever be. I am alive. And I am with Bren.

I slip on Bren's comfy flannel shirt and take a deep breath, passing through Danny's bedroom and into the living room.

Bren sits on his well-loved leather couch. On the ottoman in front of him, two barren plates rest atop of a tray beside an almost empty glass of water. He's polishing off what's left of a sandwich in a pair of cotton shorts and nothing else. His hair remains damp from the shower, curling the mounds of his wavy strands extra tight.

Bren is hot. A ruggedly handsome brute of a male I can't wait to touch.

He looks up to find me smiling. Instead of returning my smile, he simply stares, his cheeks puffed from the rather large bite in his mouth. Appearing more werechipmunk than wolf, I can't help but giggle. He swallows hard, practically choking.

I hurry into the kitchen to refill his glass, pressing my hand into the water dispenser of his stainless-steel refrigerator as the tea kettle whistles.

Bren

Emme shouldn't be here. Not with that smile and not all naked except for my shirt.

The flannel, it's too big on her. Except it might as well be a thong with how good she looks in it.

When she walked in, I couldn't stop staring at her face. Now, I can't keep my eyes off her ass.

My wolf (okay, me too, a'ight?) watch her intently as she shuts off the stove and reaches for a mug in the cupboard. The edge of the flannel trails up her backside, higher and higher, as she stretches onto the tips of her toes.

Shit.

She's not wearing panties.

The hell?

I'm not going to make it.

No way am I not going to have sex with her.

I growl. Get it together, man; this is Emme, not some one-night stand.

Emme tosses her hair as she looks behind her. "Is something wrong?"

I shake my head like a stupid mutt. It's the only thing I can do right now. Emme flashes another smile and returns to the living room. Using care, she places a glass of water and her cup of tea on the tray. She pauses, her features tender as she eases onto the couch beside me.

With her eyes locked on mine, she runs her fingertips gently through my hair, the compassion I've come to know so well casting an outpouring of emotion across her irises.

I'm trying to convince myself the affection is from one pal to another, that she'd pet a puppy she encountered on the street the same way.

Except, friends don't look at friends the way Emme is looking at me. And I'm no innocent little pup.

She leans forward and reaches for the glass of water, passing it to me with yet another one of her "Emme" smiles. "You looked thirsty," she says.

"I'm all right." It's what I say, but then I chug it.

The chill cuts it's way to my stomach, cooling me off but sure as hell not enough.

I should have poured the water into my goddamn shorts.

"Bren," she says. "Your thigh looks awful."

"What?" Between trying to live and then trying to get here, I forgot just how bad *Octobitch* messed me up. "It's fine, Emme. In another hour, I'll be all healed up."

"It's not fine," she insists. "I was too busy healing myself and never noticed how bad you were hurt. Here, let me help you."

"Emme, you don't have to."

"Yes, I do," she says.

Her soft hands slip onto my knee and gradually maneuver upward. My breath hitches. "Emme, *don't*," I rasp.

"I want to," she whispers. "There's a lot I want to do for you."

She feels her way along the banged-up muscle and bone. It feels good. Amazing. And hell, if I ain't in trouble.

I try to envision things that aren't sexual, like kite flying. It works on Little Bren as well as you might guess. Don't get me wrong. I see the kite. Except Emme is flying it naked.

I swipe my face and think of horses. Wild horses, galloping through a field of wheat. Except those damn horses only want to make me ride Emme.

Yeah, that mind over matter thing is just a bunch of bullshit. I give up on trying to relax, failing miserably.

Emme's healing yellow light surrounds me in a soft embrace. It should soothe me, like it normally does, instead it arouses me. Everything about Emme is turning me on, her hair, her face, and damn, that swell of her breast peeking through the front of the flannel.

I grip the couch, trying to keep from shaking.

"There," she says. She examines my leg. At least, I hope that's what she's looking at. "Much better."

There's not so much as a hair out of place on my thigh. It doesn't surprise me. Emme is good at this, and everything else.

What does surprise me is her hands sliding up my chest.

"I uh, healed my ribs and such," I tell her.

"I know, Bren," she replies.

She tilts her chin, closes her eyes, and leans in for a kiss.

I shift away from her. "Emme, what are you doing?" I ask, like I already don't know.

"I'm trying to return that kiss you gave me at the Watering Hole." She pauses. "Will you let me?"

She places one knee between my legs. I groan from the pressure and the way my body responds.

It's not me. It's my wolf, and maybe Little Bren, too. I swear I have nothing to do with what we do next.

I grab Emme's hips and pull her into a straddle, crashing my lips against hers.

My tongue meets her savagely.

Like the rest of her, her taste is incredible. I can't get enough. I caress her thighs and her backside and—*oh yeah*—definitely not wearing panties.

Emme's skin is warmth and silky beneath my touch. A deep moan breaks from her lips as my fingers dance along her spine. It scares the shit out of me.

I scramble up and away from her so fast; she falls back on the couch.

My shirt just barely keeps her intimate parts covered. I loom over her, shaking with need.

"What's wrong?" she gasps.

I swallow hard. "Did I hurt you? Am I hurting you?"

She rights herself, blushing. "No, no. I really like what you're doing," she says.

I start to pace, stop, and work on catching my breath. "And what exactly are we doing here?"

"We're about to make love."

"McLove?"

She covers her mouth, her hair falling around her as she laughs. As her hands drop away, she rises, approaching me slowly.

"Bren. I want to make love to you." She nibbles on her bottom lip. "And if I'm right, I think you want to make love to me, too."

"Make love? Did you just say make love? Do people even do that anymore?"

"Yes," she answers, smiling.

I shake my head, this time I do pace. "Em, I've had a lot of women ask me to do some freaky shit, but this is definitely the topper."

"Why?" she asks.

I pause. "I just don't think I have it in me."

"I have total faith in you," she purrs. She unfastens all the buttons of the shirt and lets it slide off of her arms.

My heart slams into my chest like a screen door during a tornado. I'm either having some sort of panic attack or going into cardiac arrest. She eases slowly forward, similar to a cop trying to coax a jumper down from a ledge.

"Bren," she says. "Are you all right?"

No. I'm not all right. You're standing there with your perfect body, with your perfect hair draped around your perfect shoulders. Your small pink nipples are begging to be in my mouth and your thighs are screaming to wrap around my—

I punch myself in the face, hard enough to see stars and completely freak out Emme.

Her hands clasp her chest and her eyes bulge. "Bren, what are you doing?"

"It's what I'm trying *not* to do, Emme. Do you realize your sisters are going to *kill me*? Taran will burn me to embers. Celia will claw me apart. Whatever's left over, Shayna will slice to bits!"

Emme's cheeks redden and she offers me a shy smile. "Bren, my sisters aren't here."

Her fingers thread through mine. She walks backward, leading me into the bedroom. With a press of her hands against my chest, she lays me down on my bed and climbs on top of me. I can't stop my eyes from wandering to her face and her body. She's all woman. I'm not sure when it happened, but that's what she became.

Still, it doesn't stop me from saying what I do. "You're just a kid."

"No, Bren. I'm not a kid." The strands of her hair skim over her breasts as she shakes her head. "Not anymore."

No, she's not.

I rip my off my shorts in one pull, and finally discover what it's like to touch Emme.

Chapter Eighteen

Emme

All it takes is one brush of my breasts against Bren's chest and he's all over me.

His hands, those strong, *rough* hands, drag down my back as he deepens our kiss.

No one has ever kissed me this way, and I never knew I was capable of such passion.

His tongue plays with mine and drives deep, seeking to overtake, dominate, and claim me as his.

My *touch* takes over me without consent. I reach out, devouring him in as many places as I dare to reach.

Bren

Hands run through my hair, across my chest, my stomach, and shoulders, at the same time. There are four women on top of me—no, four *Emmies*. I feel her everywhere. I want to bite her, suck her and drive deep inside her. But I'm scared. Fuck me, I'm terrified.

I don't want to hurt her. I'm out of control and I don't think I can stop.

We kiss for seemingly hours until one of her hands push mine up to her breast and her teeth find my neck.

Emme

The more daring I become, the more Bren responds to my touch. When my nibbles turn to bites, he finally touches me—*really* touches me. As I vocalize my pleasure, he stops, choosing only to kiss me.

I haven't taken many lovers, and I think I'm doing all the right things. But even before Bren stops kissing me, I sense him pull away. I lift off him, stunned when I see how terrified he appears.

"Bren, don't you like what I'm doing to you?"

Bren

Are you insane? Fuck yeah.

"Yes?" I offer.

Emme gives a wiggle and lifts her hair away so I can see her. "Then why don't you show me?" she asks.

Her hands and *touch* take hold of me once more, stroking my long, throbbing hardness.

"Please," she begs in a seductive whisper that reflects the passion swimming through her gaze. "Please show me."

Her fingertips skim down my chest and her *touch* turns aggressive, exploring every inch of me until I'm practically on fire. She tugs, strokes, bowing my back and forcing me to dig my fingers through the mattress.

She bites her bottom lip, smiling with lust as she toys with me.

Long waves of her messy hair sweep against her shoulders. Never has a woman looked so sexy, and never have I felt like this.

Her pulls are unrelenting, dire, as if she can't stop until I release.

"Emme." I gasp, grunting and speaking through my teeth. "I don't want to hurt you."

"You won't," she promises. "Please, Bren. Make us both feel good."

Emme gives me one last jerk and I explode into action. I flip her onto her back and enter her with my fingers. My teeth graze her nipples as my mouth roams her body.

She moans, beating back a scream.

She's becoming louder.

It's just not loud enough.

I spread her legs, dipping my head to taste her.

Emme bucks, jumping further down the bed. She reaches out to me, using her power to return the favor.

An invisible tongue finds me, moving down to my base and taking me fully. I like it. It's good, damn good. But she wants more.

She breaks away from me and buries her face into my lap. The scrape of teeth grazing along my thick length only doubles our lust. Emme can do no wrong.

We continue like fervent lovers, frantic to out-do the other. I moan and growl. She gasps and whimpers, pleading for me to go harder.

When I think I can't hold back anymore, she begs me to take her completely.

Emme

This is a torturous tease. There's nothing more I desire than Bren inside of me. It takes some time and maneuvering, but finally, he makes his way in.

Bren barely fits. It hurts with the most delicious pain. The rock of his hips are initially slow. As his need soars, so do his quickening thrusts.

I orgasm twice before he finishes. He collapses onto his back, his gaze feverish and his breathing mere pants. I climb on top of him and touch his soft beard.

Bren kisses me for a long time and I cherish every second. As our lips part, I rest my head against his chest and sigh in absolute bliss.

Bren

"I knew this was right," she whispers.

It's the last thing Emme says before she drifts to sleep.

This is the part where I usually say, "Okay babe, I'd better get going," or "I have to get up early. How 'bout I call you a cab?"

Yeah. It's how I roll. It's how the females I go home with roll.

So why am I letting Emme sleep on top of me? Why am I stroking her back and hoping like hell she doesn't leave?

Da fuck? Am I going to flick on the *Lifetime* channel and start crying, next? The last time I let a woman sleep with me all night, I was ten, she was my Mom, and she'd dozed off reading me a story.

Emme looks pure lying next to me. How did I never notice her this way before?

I can't wake her now. It'd be a dick move.

My fingers stop skimming down her back and I settle into her. So what if she stays one night? She was so cold before and now, she's warm and soft and peaceful. Only an asshole would disturb her now.

* * *

My landline rings next to me, waking me up from the best damn sleep of my life.

"*What?*"

"Son of a bitch, Bren, you don't have to growl."

"Taran?" I ask. I bolt upright. *She knows.*

"Yes, it's Taran. Goddamn it, you just about blew out my eardrum."

"Oh," I say.

"Oh? Really? That's all you have to say for yourself?" she demands.

"Ah."

She huffs. "Well, you probably know why I'm calling."

Emme stirs beside me and stretches. The sheet covering her slips down and exposes her breast. "It was an accident," I blurt out.

There's a rather dramatic and irate pause on the other end. "What was an accident?" she asks.

"I don't fuckin' know. Whatever you're asking about."

"The werewolf who was cut up like sushi?" she asks. "I thought some mutant octopus witch did that."

"She did," I reply.

"Then what are *you* talking about?" she bites out.

"I don't know." Clearly. "Whatever it is you want to talk about."

Here's the deal, I used to be a good liar. But with the most beloved Wird sister lying naked next to me, I'm not anymore.

Taran replies, sounding pissier than when she accused me of blowing out her eardrum. "Tell me you're day drinking, Bren. Tell me it's Witches Brew. Tell me I shouldn't light your ass up like fireworks."

"I..."

I've got nothing is what I've got.

"For hell's sake, Bren," she barks into the phone. "Get a hold of yourself and grow up, man. This is embarrassing."

And now in addition to being an alcoholic she thinks I'm a loser.

From the other end of the line, I hear her fluff her hair. "Anyway, I'm calling because no one's heard from Emme. I just got in from Iran. Gemini's pissed, something about me causing international, unconscionable, and blasphemous chaos or some nonsense. It's a total lie. The Caspian mountain only caught a little bit on fire and that sacred shrine was *really old*. It was one good windstorm from crumbling into powder, but like always, it's my fault. Can you believe that shit?"

"No," I say, although I really can. Taran and I share the same vocabulary and temper. Some have speculated as to why we never dated. This is why. We would seriously murder each other.

"Gemini's at the Den working things through with the Caspian Den. Get this, their alpha is a wereibex. An actual ibex! He almost attacked me, but then realized I was just there to save the day. Gemini insists that the only reason he didn't go all ibex on me is because my clothes were in tatters and my boobs were hanging out, but honest-to-God, even though they were, he was a decent guy."

"I'm sure he was," I say, watching Emme sit up.

"Anyway, the thing with Genevieve and the witches took forever. Shayna and Koda were about to crash or play a round of Jack Be Nimble meets Horny Humpty Dumpty or whatever the hell, and they realized Emme wasn't here. Do you think she ran out for food or something? Koda says her scent is older, from earlier last evening. Tell me you know where she is and that she's safe before we all lose our damn minds."

"Is everything all right?" Emme asks. "You seem stressed."

No biggie. I'm just about to die.

I cover the receiver with my palm, thanking heaven and back Taran doesn't have supernatural hearing and that Emme's voice is so soft.

"It's *Taran*," I whisper. "She wants to know where you are."

Emme pushes the hair from her face. She smiles and extends her palm, requesting the phone.

Damn. Does the army know about that smile? She could be our secret weapon against the terrorists.

"Hi, Taran."

"Omigod, Emme. Thank God. Are you okay?"

"I'm fine," she replies. "We were badly banged up and tired, so I stayed with Bren."

"You sound exhausted," Taran says.

She knows. Yup definitely knows.

"I just woke up," Emme says, flashing me another grin.

Taran huffs. "Well considering you spent the night kicking ass and wiping the floor with octopus parts, I can't blame you for crashing. I slept a little on the plane, after Gemini and I had makeup sex, you know how it goes."

Emme runs her fingertips down my chest. "I do, actually."

"Why didn't you call to say you were staying at Bren's?"

"Well..."

No!

I make a grab for the phone. Emme squirms away from me. For a little thing, she's really slippery.

"A lot happened last night, Taran. More than I expected considering I was only going on a date."

"No kidding," Taran replies. "Look, I'm sorry I wasn't there for you. All of us are. Celia felt so bad, she and Aric are en route home."

Taran's attention shifts. "Emme's fine. She's at Bren's. You can go back to whatever messed up nursery rhyme you're doing...What...Koda, calm down...Don't you growl at me...We tell each other everything. Why does this shock you...Just, look, don't wear that Little Bo Peep outfit around me...It's disturbing...I don't care what you do in your bedroom, I only care what I do in mine....okay, Jack and Jill then. Sorry, the dress threw me off..."

Taran returns to the call. "Damn, Koda is so sensitive. Hopefully, Shayna will sheer his ass or carry his bucket, whatever turns him on, so he'll be less cranky. I haven't slept much, but I'm pretty wired. I can come get you if you want."

"No, thank you," Emme replies. "I'm still worn out. Bren can just take me home later."

"Okay, sweetie," Taran says. "Whatever you want."

"Taran, one more thing," Emme says.

I shake my head. *Don't do it. Don't tell her. I wanna live.*

Emme pats my shoulder, speaking lightly into the phone. "Do you know what happened to the Lessers?"

"The fish and the ferret who invoked Mirror?" Taran asks.

"I believe Merche was a guinea pig," Emme clarifies. "I spoke with Genevieve about giving them a chance, but I can't be certain she will."

"Well, Emme, let's just say Genevieve did you a favor by not killing them. Had it been me pulling that crap, you know she would have come at me, wand and broomstick waving. From what Shayna said, Vieve changed the Lessers back to full humans. Vieve is returning them home for the local covens to deal with. It's a smart move. It absolves Vieve of any guilt and forces the other head witches to apologize and make amends."

"And amplifies Genevieve's reputation as a just and strong leader," Emme adds.

"Once more the great and powerful Genevieve comes out on top," I say, chuckling.

Emme drums her fingers against my thigh. "Do you think the other head witches will kill Merche and Farrah?"

TOUCH OF EVIL · 159

"I don't think they can," Taran says. "It will only make them look worse and Vieve better. My guess is they'll have to work off their penance as servants for the next decade or so. It'll suck, but it beats dying."

Emme adjusts her position beside me. "I suppose. As much as they helped me, they do have a lot to account for."

"Well, you hang with bitches, you're going to get fleas. Hey, put Bren back on, will you?"

"He's still here," Emme says, her tender smile lifting.

"Bren, thanks for taking care of Emme," Taran says. "We knew you wouldn't let anything happen to our girl."

I rub my face. *I took care of her, all right.*

"Yeah, dude," Shayna chimes into the phone. "You're the best."

From the way Emme was screaming, I sure was.

"No problem," I mutter.

Emme returns the phone to the base and looks up at me. Her hair is wild and her smile seductive. As the sheet tents on my lap, I grab her and pull her on top of me.

The moment my mouth touches hers and my hands get to wandering, she moans.

Screw it. I'm already in trouble. Might as well make the best of it.

Chapter Nineteen

Bren

The door to the apartment opens sometime later. Dan struts in, whistling, as usual.

His whistles cut off abruptly the moment he reaches the living room.

He's caught a whiff of Emme's scent.

And probably more.

I can picture him, looking at the couch and seeing that no one slept there. His frantic steps race toward his bedroom. He swears when he finds no one there. Let me tell you, Dan *never* swears.

He barrels down the hall toward my room. Instinct takes over. I bury Emme in the comforter and gather her possessively.

Dan throws open the door.

I growl, a long, deep, ferocious growl.

He blinks back at me, shocked. I'm shocked, too. The guy is my best friend for hell's sake.

Neither of us say anything. We just stare at one another.

He knows it's Emme squirming and squealing beneath me.

He knows what we did, what we kept doing, and how hard we went at it.

There's no hiding it. The smells of sex, arousal, and sweat are all over the room.

Emme gasps for air and makes her escape. She shoves the comforter low enough to expose her face and one arm.

"Bren, what?" Her cheek burns against my neck. I clutch her like she belongs to me. "Oh. Hi, Danny," she stammers.

Dan doesn't say jack, his eyes widening and his jaw slacking further open.

I get annoyed. "What are you looking at?"

"A dead wolf," he replies. He shakes his head. "Celia's going to beat the crap out of you..."

I bow my head and drag my hand through my hair. "I know, man."

"Taran is going to set you on fire..."

I drop my hand. "I get it, Dan."

"Shayna, oh...she's going to dice you into confetti..."

"Tell me something I don't know, Dan," I snap.

He frowns. "How about what the wolves are going to do to you, Bren? Have you thought about that? You know how they feel about Emme."

I straighten ever so slowly. I was too busy fearing the wrath of the Wird girls that completely forgot about their mates.

As the youngest, the wolves constantly refer to Emme as their little sister.

The bastards will be pissed that I corrupted her. The best I can hope for is a slap on the back and a "well done" from Misha.

Emme slings her free arm around me and rests her head beneath my chin. "It's okay, Bren," she whispers. "I won't let anyone hurt you."

* * *

Dan heads into the next room, muttering something about funeral arrangements. I think he's taking off but then I hear him banging around in the kitchen and preparing food. I suppose every guy on death row deserves one last good meal.

Emme hops into the shower in my room. I'm just finishing brushing my teeth when she pokes her head out from behind the curtain. "I borrowed the extra toothbrush I found. I hope you don't mind."

I shrug. "Nope. Take it with you if you want. Dan bought a few packs right before he moved out. I have enough to last me a couple of years."

The curtain crinkles as she tightens her grip. "Don't you think it's better if I leave it here?"

I rinse my mouth. "For what?"

"For next time."

My head snaps up. "Next time?"

Emme fiddles with the curtain, appearing shy. "Bren, last night, we shared something beautiful. Don't you think, love?"

Love? No. No way did she just call me that.

I pause in the middle of drying my hands, trying to find my words. Except, no words come.

They can't come.

Not after Emme just said what she did, and not with my heart thumping like it is.

I release the towel, not bothering to pick it up when it falls on the floor.

I lean against the wall just beside the shower. The tile is cold, but I barely feel it. All I sense is misery. "Emme, look, last night was really, *really* great. I mean, after we killed everything we had to kill and survived. It's just..."

"It's just what?" she asks, her voice sad.

I meet her face. It's the least I can do. "I'm not good at these things. Having a girlfriend, I mean. It's not something I've ever had before."

Emme turns off the shower and steps out. Water drips down her body, gathering in droplets around her nipples. I want to lick them dry and she knows it. Instead, I reach into the linen closet and cover her with a clean towel.

She clasps my wrists, her hope fizzling out right in front of me. "I know relationships aren't one of your strengths, and I know your life hasn't been easy," she begins.

My jaw clenches. "Emme, please don't go there. Not about my folks, okay?"

I didn't think it was possible, but her voice grows even more hurt. "I'm not trying to complicate things or make you feel bad, Bren. There's just something between us, and I think you feel it, too."

My frown deepens. "Em, I don't know what I feel."

Her gaze drops. "All right," she says. "I understand. But I'd like you to understand that having a girlfriend, a relationship, isn't something to fear."

I think back to my parents. "Yeah. Sure."

I step out of her reach but can't quite bring myself to leave the bathroom. I take in her scent. Emme smells just like a cloud might, clean and peaceful.

Too bad I messed her up like I did.

She wraps her head in that cute turban-thing like girls do, pausing as if unsure to ask what she does. "Do you like me, Bren?"

"You know I do, Emme."

She presses her lips. "I really like you, too. I didn't know how much... until last night."

"I get it, Emme. But I don't do relationships."

Damn. Here come the images of my parents again, loving on each other like they did, right up until they killed themselves and left me alone.

"It's not easy for me to have people," I remind her. "Dan, you and your sisters, you were the first." I shake my head. "Do you see how I am with the pack? We're supposed to be bros, but you and me know that'll never happen."

"Bren," she says, her voice growing strained. "There are things you've experienced that continue to haunt you, and I'm sorry. But please, don't let them keep you from enjoying the good things in life."

"Like a girlfriend?" I offer. I don't mean to be an asshole, but right now, I'm acting like one.

Emme's shoulders droop. "I'll never pressure you into something you don't want. But if you're ready for us, I'm ready, too."

I try to kiss her when she reaches up. In that kiss, I want to tell her that I'm sorry. I want to kiss away the pain I'm causing. I want to show her how important she is and how I don't really want her to go.

Emme denies me that kiss, turning away to hug me instead. It's just as well. A kiss from me was where this all started.

It's what I tell myself. But not kissing Emme feels wrong.

She loosens her grip around me. I hang on. I don't want to let her go. But I do.

Guys like me, with screwed up pasts, don't belong with the Emmies of the world.

Right?

* * *

When we sit down to eat, Emme mostly plays with her food, barely taking more than a few bites. No wonder she's so small.

I fork some sausage and lift it up to her face. "Here, you eat like a bird."

"Birds actually eat twice their weight," Dan chimes in.

"Shut up, Dan. I'm trying to keep her alive over here."

Emme giggles, and Holy God, it's like music to my ears. Maybe she doesn't hate me. Maybe everything will go back to normal between us.

She lets me feed her. I do a doubletake when I catch Dan with his jaw practically hitting the table.

I narrow my eyes at him. It's enough for him to compose himself.

Emme swallows her food and smiles at Dan. "Thank you for lending me your sweatpants, Danny."

"No problem, Emme," he says. He motions with his fork. "You're still swimming in them, but I'm sure they'll fit you better than anything Bren has."

I smirk. "That's because you have those womanly hips, whereas I have a man's body."

"These hips help me get where I'm going and that's good enough for me," Dan fires back. He wipes his mouth and folds his napkin when he sees Emme is done. "I have to get back to the Den. If you're ready, Emme, I can drop you off on my way."

"Don't even think about it, Dan," I snarl. "She's *mine*. *I'm* taking her home!"

Both regard me like I'm nuts. Can't really blame them seeing how I *changed* from werewolf to raging psycho.

I cough into my napkin. "What I mean is, I can take you home, Emme. If you, you know, want me to."

"That would be nice," Emme says slowly. She rises and makes her way to Danny. "Thank you for the meal. It was lovely."

She bends to hug him. They both jolt when I let out the mother f'ing growls of all growls.

Holy shit. I've turned into Aric Connor.

* * *

I was worried that my possessiveness scared Emme, hell, it scared me. I wasn't sure how she'd be in the car. To my shock, she leans against me, cuddling as close as we were in bed. I drape my arm around her. Although we don't speak the whole way back to Dollar Point, I keep my hold around her, wishing I didn't have to let her go.

I pull into the cul-de-sac where she lives and park in front of her house. Before I can reach her side of the car, she's already out. We walk in silence and without looking at each other. We also walk without holding hands, something that makes me feel even worse.

My guess is she wants me to say something, *anything* about us. Except that I can't.

We hop up on the front porch and wait together at the door.

Ordinarily, I'd walk inside with her, shoot the shit with her family, and maybe sit and catch a movie with them. But in one night, everything changed. I don't see myself hanging like I used to with my girls, and I swear to Christ, it breaks my damn heart.

Emme shuffles her feet. "We're planning a late dinner tonight to celebrate being home as a family again."

"Hmm," I say.

"I'm cooking," she says when I keep my trap shut. "And I'd like you to come."

See? This is what I mean. Before yesterday, she wouldn't need to ask. She would just tell me what time dinner was and I'd be there. Now, hell, I don't know what to say.

"If you don't want to, I'll suppose I'll just see you around," she says. She glances down, like girls do when they're trying not to cry. "But if you do come, then I'll know you want to give us a try."

My knuckles crack and a sting pricks along my eyes. I hate this. All of it.

"Em?"

"Yes, Bren?"

"I don't think you'll see me tonight."

She nods, quickly, trying to be braver than I can scent she feels. "All right," she says.

Emme takes a step back when I try to kiss her, and I swear it's the last punch in the gut I need. I try to tell her how sorry I am, but then the door swings open and I know I'm in trouble.

I jolt. There, as clear as day, is the head of the Wird Family.

Celia prowls through the door, her big mane of waves fluttering as she moves and the green eyes of her tigress flashing. Emme never quite understood how wickedly terrifying Celia can be.

"All right, maybe she's killed demons, vampires, *weres*, and a couple of humans, but otherwise she's really sweet," Emme always asserted.

No. Celia isn't sweet. Not when I just banged her little sister like a drummer at the Fourth of July parade.

"Hey," she says.

"Hey, Ceel." I clutch Emme by the shoulders and shove her into Celia's arms. "Well, here she is. Safe and sound."

Celia shoots me a look, it's similar to the one Emme and Dan gave me earlier. Still, she embraces Emme. "I would expect no less," she replies. "You were together, weren't you?"

"What the hell is that supposed to mean?" I snap.

Celia releases Emme slowly. She turns to me, arms crossed and eyebrows raised. Oh, and look, there's that killer predator poking through again. "What do you think it means, Bren?"

"Nothing." I back away, my hands up in surrender. "Well, gotta go."

I peel out of that neighborhood like Celia already knows. More than once I look back to see if she's following. I'm a dead man. Jesus God, I am dead.

Chapter Twenty

Bren

It's official: Dan has transformed me into a nerd. I might as well tear up my alpha male card in exchange for a library card.

I arrive back at my apartment to find Dan waiting like the mother hen that he is.

He stands, his eyes peering at the paper grocery bag in my grip. "What did you buy?"

I shrug. "Just a couple of magazines."

We wrestle for the bag when he dives for it. The bag tears and the contents spill all over the floor.

Dan blinks back at me like I'm some damn stranger. "You bought *Women's World.*"

"Yeah," I say, like it's no biggie.

"And *Redbook.* And *Glamour* an-and *Better Homes and Garden.*"

"*So what?*" I snap. "Why don't you go masturbate to women's golf and leave me the hell alone."

"I don't do that." He scowls. "Anymore."

I roll my eyes. "Whatever." I bend to swipe the magazines off the floor.

"Bren," he says, keeping me in place. "We have to talk about this morning."

"Yeah, sorry about that. I don't know why I was so pissed. Emme, I don't know, Dan. She wants to be my girlfriend and you know how I feel about that shit."

Dan blows out a breath that makes his lips motorboat. "Bren, Emme can't be your girlfriend."

This is why Dan is my best friend. I throw up my hands. "That's exactly what I was trying to tell her—"

"She's your mate," he says, cutting me off.

Complete silence fills the room. I let it, then absolutely lose my shit. *"Are you out of your mind? What the hell are you talking about?!"*

Instead of running for the hills like he damn well should, he flops onto the couch. "Bren, take a look at the way you acted this morning. You had her wrapped up in bed like she was your possession."

"I didn't want her to get cold," I say, like a moron.

"When we sat down to eat, you fed her meat," he tells me. "Just like a wolf would in the wild."

"It's like I told you, she doesn't eat enough."

Even if Dan couldn't sniff out the truth, he knows me enough to know I'm grasping at straws. "You told me she was yours, and when she tried to hug me, you all but ripped out my jugular."

"I was just tired," I mutter. "Males are cranky and unreasonable when sleep deprived."

"Face it, Bren. Your wolf has found his mate."

"No, *no.* Don't go there, Dan. Not you. Not when you know all the shit I've been through."

Dan's features grow solemn. "I'm not trying to hurt you, Bren. I know you think of matehood as more of a curse than something sacred."

"That's because it is," I bite out. "Seen Celia and Aric lately? How are they doing there, Dan?"

Dan expressions steels. "Better now that they have each other."

It was easier to shift the conversation away from my folks and onto Celia and Aric. But Dan has always been too smart for his own good.

"What about me?" I ask. "Do you know me at all? All I've done since the day we met is sleep around."

Dan shrugs, unfazed. "Maybe that was your wolf's desperate search for his other half."

I mutter a swear. "None of this makes sense. I've known Emme for years. If she was really my mate, I would have known before last night."

Dan gives it some thought, not that it slows him down. "Not necessarily. Sometimes it takes an intimate moment to trigger a wolf's recognition. Did anything different happen last night? I mean, before you actually slept together?"

"She kissed me like she always does," I reply.

"On the cheek?" he asks.

"Well, she tried. But then she accidently touched my lips with hers and then I..."

Oh shit.

Chapter Twenty-One

Emme

I place the last plate in the dishwasher and hit start. It's almost midnight and Bren never showed.

I walk into the family room, glancing toward Taran and Gemini's bedroom and then to the stairs where Celia and Shayna are likely asleep beside their mates.

Dinner was nice, as nice as it could be. As usual Shayna did most of the talking, and while my family sensed something was wrong, they gave me the space I desperately needed. It won't last. Before long, the questions will come and I'm not certain I'll be ready with answers.

I lower myself to the couch, resigned to spend another night binge watching *The Marvelous Miss Maisel* and gushing about her clothes.

No. That's a lie. There'll be no gushing, not tonight.

What I'm hoping is that there won't be any tears.

Last night was something. And now it's gone.

The doorbell rings and my heart leaps out of my chest.

It's Bren. It must be.

I scramble for the door and open it, choking on my hello.

Bren stands in front me with a bouquet of flowers wrapped in paper and tied with string. He's in a dress shirt and his best pair of jeans. I beam. Danny must have picked out his clothes.

"Hi," I say.

My smile fades when I see just how miserable he appears. He hands me the flowers.

"All the magazines said I should bring these," he mumbles. "Except for *Better Homes and Garden*. They tried to get me to grow them first. But there was also an article on how to arrange them. If you have a cup or something, I guess I can give it a shot."

I shut the door behind us and hug him. "Bren, why do you look so sad, love?"

He coughs, at least, I think he does.

I glance up, the extent of his heartache dulling his magnetic soul. This is so much worse than I thought.

"Don't call me that, Emme." He looks in the direction of the wooded path, but I doubt he really sees it.

"I've been driving for hours," he admits. "Left my place an hour before I was supposed to be here."

I clutch the flowers, crinkling the paper. "Why didn't you come?" I ask.

Bren's blue eyes, the ones that always reflect his humor, the ones so filled with passion earlier today, and the ones that fill me with joy glisten with grief. "I can't do this, Emme. Not to you, not to me. I just can't." He bows his head. "Trust me when I say, you deserve a lot more than me."

He turns away, his feet heavy as he makes his way down the steps. It's good in a way. He doesn't catch the way my tears soak the petals or sense that awful burn collecting in my throat.

He also doesn't catch the small smile I manage.

Bren may not be ready for me. But the world is ready for us.

Read on for an excerpt from

A Weird Girls Novel

Cecy Robson

Chapter One

Her name was Celia. I never saw her coming. I didn't know I'd needed her. But isn't that how love is supposed to work?

I hop downstairs. I don't mean I take the steps one or even three at a time. I mean I hop over the railing and leap from the second floor to the first, landing almost silently in a crouch, the backpack on my shoulders barely brushing against my spine.

I'm a *were*. A wolf to be exact. I can get away with leaping from landings physically, but not so much with my mother.

"Aric," she calls, turning away from the stove. "You're a *were*, not an animal. Take the stairs."

Dad looks up from reading his paper and smirks. "Listen to your mother, son."

I return his smirk and walk toward the kitchen. "Yes, sir. Sorry, Mom."

All eight burners are going on the stove. The smell of several pounds of bacon and more pounds of eggs stirred my senses when Mom first opened the fridge. Yeah, I'm *that* sensitive to smell, sight, sound, taste, and touch. And at fifteen, I'm *always* hungry.

I plop down next to my dad, allowing the pack to fall to my side. "Smells good," I say.

Dad sighs and turns the page. "It always does when your mother's in there. Not so much when we cook."

"Nope. We suck," I agree.

Mom's laugh draws my smile. My parents are supposed to lay into me and drive me crazy, force me to rebel, and scream at me when I do things they think I shouldn't. Except, jumping down a flight of stairs and leaving my mostly destroyed clothes on the floor aside, I'm a pretty decent kid with awesome parents.

I reach for the pitcher of freshly squeezed orange juice, yawning a lot louder than I intend. "Sorry," I say, yawning a second time when I fill my glass.

My knife slices into the butter the second Mom drops several pancakes on my plate. I'm ready to dig in when the scent of fresh buttercream finds my nose. Instead, I blink several times, trying to brush off my fatigue.

I didn't sleep much last night. My head spun with weird dreams that didn't make sense. I was wrenched backward and away from her. No... that's not right. *She* was ripped from *me*. They were taking her away from me. Whoever *she* was. I frown, remembering how bad it tore me up. I tried to hold on, tried to see her face. All I could make out were her delicate hands in mine. She sobbed, afraid to let go, while my eyes burned with rage-filled tears.

I was pissed and sad and...*broken*, except nothing I felt made sense. I didn't recognize her and I couldn't fathom why she meant so much to me.

The only thing I'm sure of is that a part of me left with her. And the way I feel this morning, it's still missing.

"Are you all right, son?" Dad asks.

I don't realize how hard I'm gripping my knife until I open my palm and all that's left is a warped piece of metal. My anger at losing her lingers and I took it out on the stupid knife.

"Sorry. I was..." I was what? Angry that I let some girl I didn't know go? "I didn't sleep well," I admit.

Dad folds his paper and places it aside, closely analyzing me. "Did you sleep with the window open?"

I don't remember leaving it open, but I nod when I remember how the cool spring breeze swept against my back when I stumbled into the bathroom this morning.

"There was a bad windstorm last night," Dad says, his dark eyebrows furrowing. "Earth's energy travels in the wind, as well as the memories of those long forgotten."

"The wind also carries magic," Mom quietly adds. She leaves the stove, a large pan of eggs gripped in her hand.

"Yes," Dad agrees. "A great deal of magic."

Mom scoops eggs onto Dad's plate, forming a large pile. "In the future, when the wind is that rough, I'd like you to sleep with the window closed."

The scent of cheese, carefully diced onions, and minced garlic seeps into my nose in a mouth-watering sweep. I dig into my eggs the moment the first scoop lands on my plate.

"Why?" I ask, swallowing quickly.

"You're different, son," Dad reminds me.

My chewing slows. It's the same thing I've heard all my life. Yeah, some things come easy for me. I'm stronger than older and larger *weres*. I'm a better tracker and more agile than anyone around. But I don't feel different. I'm just me, I guess.

"I'm serious, Aric." Dad tells me. "You achieved your first *change* before you were two months old. We went to sleep with an infant between us and woke with a wolf pup. *Two months*. I still don't think you comprehend the significance."

Maybe I don't. The most powerful *weres* achieve their first *change* at six months of age following a full moon. The weakest, closer to a year. If you don't *change* in the first year, you're more human and that's how you'll stay. It's something *weres* who mate with humans deal with. Not pures like us.

My fork hovers over my plate as I give Dad's words some thought. I shove the large helping quickly into my mouth when I sense him noticing. No *were* had ever before achieved a *change* at younger than six months-old. It makes me uncomfortable to be perceived as omnipotent. I'm not. Cut my head off or shoot me up with gold bullets, I'm just as dead as the next *were*. People around here forget that. They look at me like I'll single-handedly save the world, or some other impossible stunt. They fall all over themselves, cozying up to me, filling me with compliments they can't possibly mean. The kissing up, the bowing, the *groveling*...I hate it.

"There's no telling how strong you'll become or what powers you may inherit because of it," Dad says.

"I had trouble sleeping," I mumble. "It's no big deal." I don't want anyone making a big fuss over me. It bothers me more when my parents do it.

Aside from my small and close-knit circle of friends, they're the only ones who still see me as Aric, not the savior others have come to expect.

Mom scoops another large helping of eggs onto my plate. Tendrils of steam drift from the pan. "Perhaps. Perhaps not," she says. "But if you're this sensitive to what the wind carries, sleep with the window closed. I don't want to risk a mental attack, or worse, while you're at your most vulnerable."

I open my mouth to argue. It's not that I can't shut the stupid window or that I need it open. I suppose I just don't want to focus on how different I am. I'm already weird enough.

Mom jerks. I cringe. My parents sense my discomfort and move on. Not that I like what they're up to.

"Aidan, behave," Mom whispers.

"What? Can't a wolf show his mate a little affection?"

She slaps Dad's hand playfully off her backside.

I make a face. "I'm right here," I remind them. "Can't that wait until I'm gone?"

"Not at all," Dad replies.

He pulls Mom onto his lap. If she were human, Mom would have spilled the eggs across the wooden floor.

"Eat with me," Dad tells her. "You're doing too much."

Mom kisses his cheek and places the pan on the table, allowing Dad to feed her. It's a mate thing. A protective thing. I've been exposed to it a lot in my life. But it always strikes me as intimate and something I shouldn't watch. I leave the table, returning with a large serving tray topped with bacon. I frown when I find Mom's arms wrapped securely around Dad's neck. Her shoulder length, white hair brushes against his chest with how hard she clutches him.

"You're going hunting again, aren't you?" I ask.

Mom lowers her eyelids as if in pain. Dad smiles softly at her, stroking her hair until she opens her eyes. She doesn't return his smile. It bothers me to see her upset.

"What's going on?" I ask.

"There's a dark witch causing trouble in Lesotho," Dad replies, continuing his slow strokes over Mom's hair.

I reach for more bacon and eggs. "Where's that?" I ask.

"Africa," Mom replies. "It's a territory known for diamond smuggling and dark magic."

"Cue the witch," I guess. Not all witches are dark. Last summer, I met Bellissima, one of the strongest light witches of her kind, along with her daughter, Guinevere, or was it Genevieve? It was something like that. They were okay. But dark witches really suck and give *weres* plenty of problems to chase.

As Guardians of the Earth, it's our job to protect the unsuspecting human populace from things that hunt them. Those creatures that go bump in the night? *We* eat *them.*

I shove a forkful of eggs into my mouth and stab a few more pieces of bacon. "How'd you hear about the witch?" I ask.

"She's protecting the diamond smugglers in the area," Dad explains.

I feel my eyes darken and a growl build deep within me. "In exchange for what?"

Dad doesn't blink. "Sacrifices, mainly human women and children."

I look to Mom, not liking where this is headed. "The women are deeply oppressed throughout the region," she explains. "When you find women fraught with worries of violence and struggling to feed their families, they tend to be more pure of heart and intent, and therefore easier to victimize. The children..." Mom straightens, passing her fingertips along the gray peppering Dad's temple. "There's nothing more sacred than a child's soul."

"Which makes the blood sacrifices she seeks more valuable. The purer the soul, the more power each kill will grant her," I finish for her. They nod. "Can I go with you?"

"No," Mom answers at the same time Dad says, "Maybe."

I perk up, my inner wolf totally losing it. "I can go?"

Mom shoots Dad a reprimanding look. "Aric is almost of age, Eliza," Dad gently reminds her. "He's far surpassed seasoned *weres* in strength, ability, and cunning."

Mom leaves Dad's lap, taking the empty pan with her. "No," she says.

Dad and I exchange glances. I know better than to speak up. Mom walks to the large porcelain sink and dumps the pan, gripping the edge.

"Our world isn't what it once was," she says. "It's changing in ways even the wisest among us never predicted, Aidan."

Dad gets up slowly, briefly pausing behind her before his hands encircle her waist. He kisses her shoulder. "The world is changing," he agrees. "But it's our duty to maintain it, so good continues to prevail."

"There are many *weres* across the globe now," she reminds him. "Unlike generations ago, when our kind struggled to breed and flourish." She looks up at Dad, her soft brown eyes pleading. "Request that another pack or Leader go in your place. I hate it when you hunt. I hate it when you leave me. Please, my love, don't take our son, too."

"All right," he tells her.

"Wait," I interrupt. "Don't I get a say?" I don't know who's more bummed, me or my wolf.

Dad turns around, keeping Mom against him. "I need you here to protect your mother," he says.

I raise my eyebrows at him. He grins and so does Mom. She's almost sixty and Dad is seventy-five. Although they tried, they didn't have me until late in life. That doesn't mean either couldn't wipe the floor with anyone who messed with them. And if I wasn't around, Mom would be the one hunting alongside Dad, just as they did for years before I came along.

"Aric," Dad says. "I'm not yet sure I'm going. There's already a local pack assigned to track and kill the witch." He looks at my mother. "But in the chance I go, I won't upset your mother further by taking you along."

"Nothing's going to happen to you," I insist. "And if I'm with you, nothing will happen to us."

I mean what I say. My dad is unstoppable. A king among *weres* and my hero.

Dad offers a lopsided smile. "Aric, your mother is worried enough."

"I know, but—"

"*Especially* with all those females knocking on our door, seeking your company," he interrupts.

I roll my eyes. The females I know are annoying at best, looking to get with me for all the wrong reasons. "I don't even like them."

Dad barks out a laugh. "Not yet. But you will, son. It's just a matter of time."

"I just hope it's not any time soon," Mom quietly adds. She's still upset.

I rise, recognizing they need time. "Where you off to?" Dad asks.

"Hunting," I reply, excited for our plans and that we finally get a few days off from school. "Liam swears he scented elk near Mount Elbert."

Dad leads Mom forward, his fingers threaded in hers. "Is it just you and Liam?" he asks.

"No. Gemini is coming and so is Koda."

Mom exchanges a worried glance with Dad. "How is Miakoda?" she asks.

I shrug. When it comes to Koda, I walk a fine line between betraying my friend and keeping things from my parents. For the most part, I'm allowed free rein. They trust me, and I want to keep things that way. So, I tell them just enough to stay true to my friend.

"Koda's all right. He mostly stays at Liam's. The other night, he was with Gem."

Dad's voice grows an edge. "Do I need to pay his father a visit?"

My gaze lowers to the floor to hide my growing resentment of Koda's father. Except, resentment, anger, *any* emotion carries a scent my folks will recognize as easily as they take their next breath. It's the reason *weres* are so good at sniffing out lies.

Koda's relationship with his dad isn't like mine. Where I'd take a spray of gold bullets to keep my parents safe, Koda would run the other way with tears of agony mixed with relief likely streaming down his face.

"Aric," Dad says, his tone more severe. "Is Koda's father hurting him or his mother?"

"No," I answer truthfully. But only because Koda hasn't been around to let him.

Dad is a pureblood and Leader, just like Mom and just like me. Dad is also our pack alpha, the one who oversees *weres* and their activity within his territory. As formidable as he is, he's often tasked with solving matters outside our region that other *weres* can't handle. But his responsibilities

are first and foremost to his pack. The same pack Koda and his family belong to.

"Aric," Dad says, this time more gently. "I'm only trying to help
Koda and keep him and his family safe."

"I know." I meet my father square in the eyes, something most *weres*
wouldn't dare do. "I'll try to talk to him today and see where he's at."

Dad nods, but he doesn't appear any less concerned. I can't blame
him. Not after everything Koda's been through.

"Tell Miakoda he always has a home with us," Mom says.

"I will. Thanks, Mom."

My wolf stiffens when I bend to hug her. We have company. I release
her slowly and turn toward the front of the house, my excitement building when I hear the voices of my friends.

"They're here," I say. "Gotta go."

"Be careful," Mom says.

I grin. "I'm going hunting, Mom. What could happen?"

I glide down the steep incline on four paws, digging my claws into the
thick forest bed to keep my balance. The weight of my three-hundred-
pound wolf form leaves deep indentations in the soil. There wasn't just
one elk. There was a massive herd. We separated them as a pack, targeting
the eldest and weakest, as nature demands.

The one I'm chasing stumbles down the ravine, his immense body
crashing into the river bank and sending waves of muddy water to
drench my face. I shake off the thick drops blinding me and hurtle forward. I'm almost on him, my excitement of snapping his neck and bring-
ing home a feast propelling me faster.

I bare my teeth at the scent of his fear. Despite his weariness, he's
fighting the kill. I can respect him as my prey. That doesn't mean I'll let
him go. My supernatural strength jets me faster, ghosting over the slippery rocks when the elk stumbles. He quickly recovers on wobbly limbs.
It doesn't matter. I have him. My family will have a sweet meal tonight.

We round the bend as I leap toward his neck. My fangs barely graze
his tough pelt before I crash into what feels like an invisible wall. The

force flings me backward, slamming me into the river bed. I whirl up, wondering what happened, and *pissed* that it did.

The sound of beating hooves grows distant as the elk disappears. I ignore his escape and growl with murderous rage.

Something's here. Something different. Something magical.

My paws keep my footing over the uneven and rocky bank as I stalk forward. I poke at the air with my nose, trying to sense the wall or whatever it was that caused my fall.

My nose twitches, latching onto something...*weird*. It's not elk, not deer, not even rabbit.

I smell predator.

A challenging growl rumbles through my torso and down my legs, causing a ripple across the water. My eyes sweep my surroundings, up the incline where the woods are thickest and back down where small, gentle waves splash over the river rocks.

Where are you? I growl again.

I angle my body to the left and frown. Something like rot permeates from the forest. It reeks of dead prey and danger, but then it moves further away from me and the predator I seek.

My eyes round with surprise when I hone in on a different scent. In the breeze, cascading along the bank, the fragrance of water misting over roses overtakes the aroma of pine, rich soil, and thick beds of moss, ensnaring me in its beauty.

An excited chill runs down my spine, standing my fur on end. I shake my head, trying to clear a scent that has no business latched to another predator...especially one warning me to keep my distance.

My ears perk up and my eyes fix on a thick mound of blackberry brambles a few feet away.

There you are...

I prowl forward, my steps quiet and purposeful and my jaws set to sink into bone.

This isn't a cougar. They run from us.

This is hungry.

Dangerous.

Weird.

184 · CECY ROBSON

My body quivers with growing excitement and my thunderous growls echo. I snap my jaws in challenge, letting my prey know I sense him.

It's time to flee or fight. The choice is his. I'm not going anywhere.

The brush shifts. Slowly, very slowly, my prey rises. My lips peel back, yet the next growl dissipates before it can fully form.

Instead of fur, wet, wavy brown hair with streaks of gold catch the faint sunlight, spilling over slender shoulders and flawless olive skin, while droplets of river water trickle around large green eyes and full pink lips.

I stop breathing.

She's young.

My age.

And she's naked.

READER'S GUIDE TO THE MAGICAL WORLD
OF THE WEIRD GIRLS SERIES

acute bloodlust A condition that occurs when a vampire goes too long without consuming blood. Increases the vampire's thirst to lethal levels. It is remedied by feeding the vampire.

Call The ability of one supernatural creature to reach out to another, through either thoughts or sounds. A vampire can pass his or her *call* by transferring a bit of magic into the receiving being's skin.

Change To transform from one being to another, typically from human to beast, and back again.

chronic bloodlust A condition caused by a curse placed on a vampire. It makes the vampire's thirst for blood insatiable and drives the vampire to insanity. The vampire grows in size from gluttony and assumes deformed features. There is no cure.

claim The method by which a werebeast consummates the union with his or her mate.

clan A group of werebeasts led by an Alpha. The types of clans differ depending on species. Werewolf clans are called "packs." Werelions belong to "prides."

Creatura The offspring of a demon lord and a werebeast.

dantem animam A soul giver. A rare being capable of returning a master vampire's soul. A master with a soul is more powerful than any other vampire in existence, as he or she is balancing life and death at once.

dark ones Creatures considered to be pure evil, such as shape-shifters or demons.

demon A creature residing in hell. Only the strongest demons may leave to stalk on earth, but their time is limited; the power of good compels them to return.

demon child The spawn of a demon lord and a mortal female. Demon children are of limited intelligence and rely predominantly on their predatory instincts.

demon lords (*demonkin*) The offspring of a witch mother and a demon. Powerful, cunning, and deadly. Unlike demons, whose time on earth is limited, demon lords may remain on earth indefinitely.

den A school where young werebeasts train and learn to fight in order to help protect the earth from mystical evil.

Elder One of the governors of a werebeast clan. Each clan is led by three Elders: an Alpha, a Beta, and an Omega. The Alpha is the supreme leader. The Beta is the second in command. The Omega settles disputes between them and has the ability to calm by releasing bits of his or her harmonized soul, or through a sense of humor muddled with magic. He possesses rare gifts and is often volatile, selfish, and of questionable loyalty.

force Emme Wird's ability to move objects with her mind.

gold The metallic element; it was cursed long ago and has damaging effects on werebeasts, vampires, and the dark ones. Supernatural creatures cannot hold gold without feeling the poisonous effects of the curse. A bullet dipped in gold will explode a supernatural creature's heart like a bomb. Gold against open skin has a searing effect.

grandmaster The master of a master vampire. Grandmasters are among the earth's most powerful creatures. Grandmasters can recognize whether the human he or she *turned* is a master upon creation. Grandmasters usually kill any master vampires they create to consume their power. Some choose to let the masters live until they become a threat, or until they've gained greater strength and therefore more consumable power.

Hag Hags, like witches, are born with their magic. They have a tendency for mischief and are as infamous for their instability as they are their power.

keep Beings a master vampire controls and is responsible for, such as those he or she has *turned* vampire, or a human he or she regularly feeds from. One master can acquire another's keep by destroying the master the keep belongs to.

Leader A pureblood werebeast in charge of delegating and planning attacks against the evils that threaten the earth.

Lesser witch Title given to a witch of weak power and who has not yet mastered control of her magic. Unlike their Superior counterparts, they aren't given talismans or staffs to amplify their magic because their control over their power is limited.

Lone A werebeast who doesn't belong to a clan, and therefore is not obligated to protect the earth from supernatural evil. Considered of lower class by those with clans.

master vampire A vampire with the ability to *turn* a human vampire. Upon their creation, masters are usually killed by their grandmaster for power. Masters are immune to fire and to sunlight born of magic, and typically carry tremendous power. Only a master or another lethal preternatural can kill a master vampire. If one master kills another, the surviving vampire acquires his or her power, wealth, and keep.

mate The being a werebeast will love and share a soul with for eternity.

Misericordia A plea for mercy in a duel.

moon sickness The werebeast equivalent of bloodlust. Brought on by a curse from a powerful enchantress. Causes excruciating pain. Attacks a werebeast's central nervous system, making the werebeast stronger and violent, and driving the werebeast to kill. No known cure exists.

mortem provocatio A fight to the death.

North American Were Council The governing body of *weres* in North America, led by a president and several council members.

potestatem bonum "The power of good." That which encloses the earth and keeps demons from remaining among the living.

Purebloods (aka *pures*) Werebeasts from generations of *were*-only family members. Considered royalty among werebeasts, they carry the responsibilities of their species. The mating between two purebloods is the only way to guarantee the conception of a *were* child.

rogue witch a witch without a coven. Must be accounted for as rogue witches tend to go one of two ways without a coven: dark or insane.

shape-shifter Evil, immortal creatures who can take any form. They are born witches, then spend years seeking innocents to sacrifice to a dark deity. When the deity deems the offerings sufficient, the witch casts a baneful spell to surrender his or her magic and humanity in exchange for immortality and the power of hell at their fingertips. Shape-shifters can command any form and are the deadliest and strongest of all mystical creatures.

Shift Celia's ability to break down her body into minute particles. Her gift allows her to travel beneath and across soil, concrete, and rock. Celia can also *shift* a limited number of beings. Disadvantages include not being able to breathe or see until she surfaces.

Skinwalkers Creatures spoken of in whispers and believed to be *weres* damned to hell for turning on their kind. A humanoid combination of animal and man that reeks of death, a *skinwalker* can manipulate the elements and subterranean arachnids. Considered impossible to kill.

solis natus magicae The proper term for sunlight born of magic, created by a wielder of spells. Considered "pure" light. Capable of destroying non-master vampires and demons. In large quantities may also kill shape-shifters. Renders the wielder helpless once fired.

Superior Witch A witch of tremendous power and magic who assumes a leadership role among the coven. Wears a talisman around her neck or carries staff with a precious stone at its center to help amplify her magic.

Surface Celia's ability to reemerge from a shift.

susceptor animae A being capable of taking one's soul, such as a vampire.

Trudhilde Radinka (aka *Destiny*) A female born once every century from the union of two witches who possesses rare talents and the aptitude to predict the future. Considered among the elite of the mystical world.

turn To transform a human into a werebeast or vampire. Werebeasts *turn* by piercing the heart of a human with their fangs and transferring a part of their essence. Vampires pierce through the skull and into the brain to transfer a taste of their magic. Werebeasts risk their lives during the *turning* process, as they are gifting a part of their souls. Should the transfer fail, both the werebeast and human die. Vampires risk nothing since they're not losing their souls, but rather taking another's and releasing it from the human's body.

vampire A being who consumes the blood of mortals to survive. Beautiful and alluring, vampires will never appear to age past thirty years. Vampires are immune to sunlight unless it is created by magic. They are also immune to objects of faith such as crucifixes. Vampires may be killed by the destruction of their hearts, decapitation, or fire. Master vampires or vampires several centuries old must have both their hearts and heads removed or their bodies completely destroyed.

vampire clans Families of vampires led by master vampires. Masters can control, communicate, and punish their keep through mental telepathy.

velum A veil conjured by magic.

virtutem lucis "The power of light." The goodness found within each mortal. That which combats the darkness.

Warrior A werebeast possessing profound skill or fighting ability. Only the elite among *weres* are granted the title of Warrior. Warriors are duty-bound to protect their Leaders and their Leaders' mates at all costs.

werebeast A supernatural predator with the ability to *change* from human to beast. Werebeasts are considered the Guardians of the Earth against mystical evil. Werebeasts will achieve their first *change* within six months to a year following birth. The younger they are when they first *change,* the more powerful they will be. Werebeasts also possess the ability to heal their wounds. They can live until the first full moon following their one hundredth birthday. Werebeasts may be killed by destruction of their hearts, decapitation, or if their bodies are completely destroyed. The only time a *were* can partially *change* is when he or she attempts to *turn* a human. A *turned* human will achieve his or her first *change* by the next full moon.

witch A being born with the power to wield magic. They worship the earth and nature. Pure witches will not take part in blood sacrifices. They cultivate the land to grow plants for their potions and use staffs and talismans to amplify their magic. To cross a witch is to feel the collective wrath of her coven.

witch fire Orange flames encased by magic, used to assassinate an enemy. Witch fire explodes like multiple grenades when the intended victim nears the spell. Flames will continue to burn until the target has been eliminated.

zombie Typically human bodies raised from the dead by a necromancer witch. It's illegal to raise or keep a zombie and is among the deadliest sins in the supernatural world. Their diet consists of other dead things such as roadkill and decaying animals

Photo by Kate Gledhill of
Kate Gledhill Photography

Cecy Robson (also writing as Rosalina San Tiago for the app Hooked) is an international and multi-award-winning author of over twenty-five character driven novels. A registered nurse of eighteen years, Cecy spends her free time creating magical worlds, heart-stopping romance, and young adult adventure. After receiving two RITA® nominations, the Maggie Award, the Award of Excellence, and a National Reader's Choice Award nomination, you can still find Cecy laughing, crying, and cheering on her characters as she pens her next story.

www.cecyrobson.com
Facebook.com/Cecy.Robson.Author
instagram.com/cecyrobsonauthor
twitter.com/cecyrobson
www.goodreads.com/CecyRobsonAuthor

For exclusive information and more, join my Newsletter!
https://cecyrobson.com/newsletter.html

Made in the USA
Coppell, TX
20 September 2020

38320520R00114